"*I see you've made up your mind,*" *Tessa stated.*

"Made up my mind?"

"Yes—to amuse yourself at my expense."

"Wouldn't it have been a mutual amusement?" Sandro enquired.

"For your information, I go in for slightly more conventional ways of getting to know men than leaping into bed with them," Tessa informed him icily.

"Grow up, Tessa," Sandro snapped. "I'm experienced enough to know when I've a responsive woman in my arms."

KATE PROCTOR is part Irish and part Welsh, though she spent most of her childhood in England and several years of her adult life in Central Africa. Now divorced, she lives just outside London with her two cats, Florence and Minnie, presented to her by her two daughters who live fairly close by. Having given up her career as a teacher on her return to England, Kate now devotes most of her time to writing. Her hobbies include crossword puzzles, bridge and, at the moment, learning Spanish.

KATE PROCTOR

A Passionate Deceit

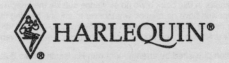

HARLEQUIN®

TORONTO • NEW YORK • LONDON
AMSTERDAM • PARIS • SYDNEY • HAMBURG
STOCKHOLM • ATHENS • TOKYO • MILAN • MADRID
PRAGUE • WARSAW • BUDAPEST • AUCKLAND

ISBN 0-373-18689-4

A PASSIONATE DECEIT

First North American Publication 1998.

CHAPTER ONE

'I THOUGHT you said the film crew would already be here,' said Tessa Conway, her wide-spaced blue eyes scanning the luxury of her almost deserted surroundings before returning to the petite figure of her cousin in the armchair beside her.

'They're here all right,' Babs Morgan assured her. 'In fact, they've already started filming on the beach just below here.' She smiled indulgently as her cousin leapt excitedly to her feet and raced to one of the several tall windows overlooking the sea in the hotel lounge. 'Tess, if you're going to behave like a demented groupie I'll take you straight back to London with me tomorrow!'

Tessa returned to her chair, an impish grin dancing across her strikingly attractive features. 'What, and let the wardrobe take care of itself?' she teased.

'I'm sure Carla, the production secretary, would be quite happy to help out should the need arise,' murmured Babs with arch innocence.

'You're not being fair, expecting me to be as blasé as you are,' laughed Tessa. 'OK, so your job brings you into constant contact with film legends and their talented offspring, but you have to remember that despite all the times you've let me help with wardrobe work I've never been within a mile of a film set.'

'Tess, I know—and I'm eternally grateful that you were able to help me out like this,' said Babs, then gave her a wicked grin. 'But, as I've already explained, all

5

the real filming's finished—so I'm afraid there won't be any stars around for you to gawp at.'

'Babs, you know I'm not the gawping type!' exclaimed Tessa indignantly. 'And I promise to be on my best behavior in the presence of anyone even remotely connected with the crew.'

'I'm only teasing, love,' murmured Babs, her expression affectionate. 'In fact, I was hoping that this little experience might start you thinking about coming to work for us permanently,' she added tentatively.

'I—that's sweet, of you,' stammered Tessa, reeling from the feelings of guilt suddenly bombarding her. 'But it's still journalism for me.'

'Tess, why can't you just accept that your stepfather's too powerful a man for you to waste your life trying to prove him wrong?' sighed Babs.

'Charles *is* wrong! Just because he owns Conway Press and has a stake in several daily papers, it doesn't mean he's infallible! All I need is a break.'

'You know, Tess,' sighed Babs, 'I sometimes get the feeling that the only thing that makes you so keen on journalism is the fact that Charles is against it.'

'Against it? He won't even discuss it with me,' protested Tessa, 'yet he puts every obstacle he can in my way—' She broke off, guilt flaring once more in her as she realised how intently she was being scrutinised. 'What's wrong?' she asked defensively.

'I knew there was something odd with you!' exclaimed Babs, grinning. 'You look about twelve. For heaven's sake, Tess, what have you done to your hair?'

Tessa's hands rose to the bunches into which she had tied her shoulder-length, dark blonde hair, her look of uncertainty as she did so making her indeed look extremely young.

'I—it's easier to manage like this,' she stammered, then gave a diffident shrug. 'Actually, I hadn't the faintest idea what sort of things people wear around a film set—I mean, they can hardly flit around the place dolled up to the nines—and you'd already left for here by the time I got around to thinking about it.'

'An Irish beach in the middle of winter is hardly the place for anyone to be dolled up to the nines!' observed Babs, then leaned back in her chair, giggling weakly. 'Tess, you haven't by any chance been reading what the gossip columnists have to say about a certain film director by the name of Sandro Lambert, have you?'

'What on earth is that supposed to mean?'

'Because, according to them, he has a gargantuan appetite for women,' laughed Babs. 'But I'm sure they'd tell you that pigtails won't help you—that he'd gobble little girls like you up for breakfast, if he felt so inclined.'

'Ha, ha,' muttered Tessa, now suddenly not in the least sure that her decision to play down her looks had not subconsciously had something to do with what she had read of Sandro Lambert's infamous reputation.

'You needn't worry, love,' teased Babs, rising to her feet and strolling over to one of the windows. 'Rumour has it that Sandro's off women with a vengeance at the moment—or, at least, that he was when filming finished a few weeks ago.'

Tessa rose and joined her, a sigh of awed disbelief escaping her as she looked out over the hotel grounds and down on to the turbulent majesty of the sea below.

'It's so incredibly wild and beautiful here,' she sighed.

'I've never been to Ireland before, but I'd love to—Babs, who's that?' she exclaimed as a tall, dark-haired woman appeared round the side of the building. 'Wow, she certainly matches the scenery for beauty!'

'Good heavens, it's Angelica Bellini!' gasped Babs, her neck craning as the woman disappeared from view.

'Is she a film star?'

Babs shook her head dismissively. 'Her brother, Umberto, often works with Sandro. He's quite a famous cameraman—you might have heard of him. There was a terrible accident on the set of Sandro's last film and Umberto was badly injured. Oh, look—here come the crew now.'

Tessa leaned forward, peering intently through the window as a group of men, laden with equipment, appeared from the shrubbed path leading up from the beach and walked across the lawn. 'Which one is Sandro Lambert?' she demanded, feeling a sudden twinge of excitement even though none of the men she could see seemed to bear any resemblance to the photographs she had seen of the fêted film director.

'He doesn't appear to be with them,' muttered Babs. 'Oh, yes—there he is now.'

Tessa watched the tall figure of a man stride from the path and across the lawn. He was dressed in what she took to be ski-wear—a sensible choice, she decided, given the piercing cold of the January wind now whipping its way through the curling blackness of his hair—his broad shoulders hunched against the elements and his hands rammed deep into his pockets. The photographs she had seen of him, she now realised, had given little indication of the true size of the man, or of the virile strength almost radiating from that purposefully striding figure. It was when he drew close enough for his features to become clearly visible that she heard her own gasp of disbelief.

'He's not exactly what you'd call photogenic, is he?' she breathed. 'Babs, he's…he's absolutely gorgeous!'

'This is all I need!' groaned Babs, hauling her away from the window and back to where they had been sitting. 'It's bad enough Angelica turning up here, but if you start drooling over him, my girl, he'll make mincemeat out of you—I mean it, Tess.'

'For heaven's sake!' exclaimed Tessa indignantly. 'I wasn't drooling! And why is it bad that Angelica's turned up?'

'I…oh, forget it,' muttered Babs. 'Look, they'll be here any moment now and I forgot to warn you not to mention your connection with Conway Press. Sandro's become a bit paranoid about the Press of late—and that's putting it mildly.'

Tessa felt her entire body tense. 'Conway Press is hardly the gutter press,' she muttered, her tone verging on defensive. 'But, if it makes you feel better, you can introduce me as Tessa Morgan.' The instant she had made the suggestion she was sickened by her own duplicity and suddenly she was no longer sure that this fortuitous trip to Ireland would turn out to be the brilliant career move it had so recently seemed.

'Actually, that's not a bad idea!' exclaimed Babs. 'It can be your professional name,' she teased.

Realising that she couldn't bring herself to deceive her cousin like this, Tessa opened her mouth to protest, then closed it with a silent groan of frustration as a group of men burst into the room, all talking at the tops of their voices in a baffling assortment of languages.

'*Ciao*, Babs!' called out one of them, a thick-set, craggily attractive man who made his way over to them with a broad grin of delight. 'This Ireland!' he groaned through a heavy Italian accent. 'So beautiful, but so wet and cold!'

'Paolo, I'd like you to meet my cousin, Tessa—Tessa Morgan,' said Babs, once she had extricated herself from his bear-hug of a greeting, her laughing emphasis of the surname leaving Tessa once again awash with feelings of guilt. 'She's standing in for my assistant who, like everyone else, has come down with the flu.'

'More of this terrible flu,' murmured Paolo with a doleful shake of his head as he and Tessa shook hands. 'We'll all die here,' he added dramatically, kneeling down in front of the huge, open fire and spreading his arms as though about to hurl himself into its flames. 'I tell Sandro the film is perfect, is finished—but he don't listen. He brings us here to freeze to death while we film footage we don't even need.'

'Paolo's the director of photography and just about the most brilliant cameraman around,' Babs confided in a loud stage whisper, 'but he's also an unremitting pessimist.'

As the rest of the group gradually joined them by the fire, Tessa felt a glow of exhilaration as she was drawn into their boisterous, multi-lingual banter, and decided that, even if her plan to break into journalism by means of a covert profile on Sandro Lambert came to nothing, at least she was going to enjoy these few days in this easygoing, cosmopolitan company.

'What we are now about to have is an Irish tea.'

Tessa turned her head at the sound of those words, attracted by their fascinatingly husky tones and the faintest trace of an accent so elusive she wasn't certain it actually existed. The first thing to catch her eye was a five-tier trolley being wheeled in by one of the hotel maids, its lower tiers laden with a lavish assortment of sandwiches, home-baked fruit breads and cream cakes, its upper ones with tea and coffee, silverware, cutlery and crockery. Her gaze then moved along to the man who had spoken and who was now conducting a conversation in Italian with Paolo and another of the men.

He had changed, she noted, completely oblivious of the intensity of her gaze as her eyes moved up from the long, perfectly shaped legs, now encased in denim so faded it was almost white, to the heavy navy fisherman's sweater adorning an athletic, broad-shouldered torso. When her gaze finally alighted on Sandro Lambert's face, the thought that again crossed her mind was that he really wasn't in the least photogenic. True, any pictures she had seen of him had portrayed an extremely good-looking man, but not one of them had managed to capture anything of the extraordinary vitality he exuded—a powerful, almost animal magnetism that seemed to radiate from him.

Tessa's eyes were still engrossed in their inspection when he broke off his conversation with the two men.

'I'm sure we can manage to serve ourselves,' she heard him tell the maid, a hint of laughter further warming the husky attractiveness of his voice.

So this was what was meant by charisma, thought Tessa, utterly fascinated and so lost in her leisurely inspection of this phenomenon possessing it that she hadn't noticed the point at which he switched from Italian to French, her whole attention caught up in the husky softness of the sounds emanating with such fluid ease from a large, expressive and sensuously full-lipped mouth that parted every now and then to display teeth of stunningly white perfection.

She would no doubt have indulged herself in an equally leisurely inspection of the strong, classical lines of his nose had her gaze not been drawn, as though by command, to a pair of eyes trained implacably on her own. The eyes she encountered were a startling blend of velvety brown and topaz, but it wasn't their unusual colour that startled her, nor was it the fact that he was still holding an animated conversation with one of the French members of his crew even while his eyes held hers in their mesmerising gaze. It was the unmitigated hostility with which she was being observed that startled her into a flustered awareness of how blatantly she had been staring.

The sensation of hot colour flaring to her cheeks only adding to her feelings of utter mortification, Tessa hastily transferred her gaze to the trolley the maid had wheeled round to the side of the sofa.

'Right, there's tea or coffee,' announced Babs. 'Which one of you is going to pour?'

There were six men in the room: Sandro Lambert standing, Paolo crouched by the hearth and practically in the fire, two sprawled along a sofa and the remaining two draped across armchairs—to a man they were looking at Babs as though she had suggested something faintly indecent.

'Just look at them, will you?' groaned Babs, trying unsuccessfully to hide her amusement. 'They're useless! Mind you, I blame Carla—Sandro's production secretary—she mothers them as though they were all three-year-olds! By the way, where is Carla?' she asked, addressing the director. 'I thought she was due here this morning.'

'She was,' sighed Sandro, approaching the trolley with the air of one condemned. 'But she's gone down with this wretched flu—as have Gina and Andy, half the grips and our continuity clerk, to mention but a few.' He gingerly lifted the lid of the hot-water jug and swore as he burned his fingers. 'Who's for tea and who's for coffee?'

'Oh, for heaven's sake, let me do it!' exclaimed Babs, shaking her head but grinning broadly as she got to her feet. 'And while we're on the subject of being short-handed, you know I have to leave tomorrow and that one of my assistants was to take charge.'

'*Was* to take charge?' enquired the director, glancing cursorily in Tessa's direction.

'Yes, was,' said Babs. 'She's also been stricken by this flu, which is why I've had to rope in my cousin. The trouble is that she's had no experience on set, so I was relying on Carla keeping an eye on things—especially the crowd scenes.'

'Your cousin?' muttered Sandro, this time not even giving Tessa a cursory look.

'Yes—Tessa Morgan,' stated Babs, again with emphasis, as she busied herself at the trolley.

'I'm resigned to the fact that things will be chaotic here without Carla,' stated Sandro gloomily, not so much by a flicker of an eyelid acknowledging Tessa's presence, 'and that our being so short-handed will only make a bad situation worse. Paolo's due to start something in Florence in ten days and anyway my schedule's too tight for any changes...so it looks as though I'll have to scrap the additional medieval crowd sequences.'

'So much for the trailer arriving any minute now, with costumes for two or three hundred,' chuckled Babs, handing him two cups of coffee. 'But at least Tess shouldn't have any problem coping with the rest.'

'The only wardrobe we'll need will be for the scenes with the old man and his sons,' said Sandro, looking down at the cups in his hands as though uncertain what to do with them. He glanced behind him and promptly handed one of them to the man nearest him, then removed himself to the chair Babs had just vacated and began drinking from the second.

'Come and get it!' called out Babs, flashing the unconcerned director a murderous look before picking up two cups of tea and handing one to Tessa. 'You don't mind if I perch here, do you?' she asked, her pointed words bringing no discernible reaction from the man at whom their sarcastic content had been directed as she sat herself down on the arm of Tessa's chair.

'Would you like me to hand round the food?' offered Tessa, once the men had helped themselves to drinks.

'Over my dead body,' growled Babs, then began chuckling to herself as two of the younger men stirred themselves and started passing the laden plates around.

'You see,' murmured Sandro after a while, amusement glinting in those extraordinary eyes of his as they homed in on Babs, 'we're not completely helpless without Carla.' Then he added with a morose sigh, 'At least, not as far as handing around a few plates goes.'

'Surely you can learn to cope without her for the short while you'll be here!' exclaimed Babs unsympathetically.

'You know perfectly well how invaluable she is to me,' he protested. 'It's like losing my right hand!'

As he went on to extol his missing production secretary in lavish terms, Tessa listened with only half an ear, her ego reeling from the completeness with which she had been ignored...and was still being ignored! Though that was a bit like wanting to have it both ways, she admitted reluctantly to herself. She was the first to complain when, as frequently happened, she found herself on the receiving end of far too enthusiastic interest from men she barely knew. In fact, she reminded herself with a squirm of embarrassment, there had been times when she had treated ogling strangers in pretty much the same way as Sandro Lambert was now treating her!

'For heaven's sake, Sandro, you can't start importing secretaries!' exclaimed Babs, her incredulous laughter distracting Tessa from her discomfiting thoughts. 'Why don't you try roping in Angelica? I'm sure she'd be only too pleased to be able to help.'

'This isn't a joking matter,' snapped Sandro. 'How am I supposed—?' He broke off as the hotel porter approached.

'Miss Morgan?'

'Yes?' said Babs, turning.

'The trailer's arrived with your costumes.'

'Thanks, I'll be right out,' she replied, draining her cup as she rose. 'Come along, Tess, duty calls.'

Tessa rose and returned her cup and saucer to the trolley, then she followed her cousin to the door.

'Heck, why didn't I think of it?' exclaimed Babs, leaning over to peer round her approaching cousin as she called out to the director who was staring morosely down into the contents of his cup. 'Sandro, I suggest you try talking nicely to Tess...she's a whiz-kid when it comes to shorthand and typing!'

Tessa gave her cousin a look of stunned incredulity.

'Is that true?' demanded Sandro, appearing as though by magic at her side and now interest personified as he gazed down at her, a megawatt smile adorning his handsome features.

'Sandro, not now,' groaned Babs, grabbing Tessa by the arm and pulling her through the door. 'I have to show Tess exactly what you'll be needing from the trailer, otherwise you'll have even more problems than you already have.'

'And what, exactly, was all that about?' hissed Tessa as she followed in her cousin's rushed wake through the rear of the hotel and out to the car park housing the equipment trailers.

'Sandro's fretting because he won't have Carla to tie his shoe-laces for him,' retorted Babs with a laugh. 'Though, as Carla never stops taking notes while he's on set, he probably does need secretarial assistance of some sort—and I'd jump at it, if I were you.' She opened up one of the trailers and motioned Tessa to follow her inside.

'I wouldn't have the faintest idea what a production secretary does,' protested Tessa.

'I'm sure Sandro's perfectly capable of explaining what he needs,' chuckled Babs, turning on a light and casting a critical eye around the neatly packed interior. 'It's just that getting three men costumed up isn't exactly going to occupy much time and I know for a fact that Sandro would pay you top rates if you stood in for Carla.' She turned and gave Tessa a reassuring smile. 'At least give it some thought while we root out what you'll need from this lot.'

* * *

'So, have you had any thoughts?' asked Babs as they ascended the main staircase to their rooms an hour later.

'It's not as though I've been offered anything yet,' stalled Tessa—but if she were, it would be a golden opportunity, she thought with an inevitable pang of guilt.

'Look, Tess, you're obviously aware how fond I am of Sandro,' said Babs gently. 'This is the third of his films I've been involved with and I've nothing but admiration for his incredible talent and also his professionalism.'

'But?' demanded Tessa wryly as they reached the door of her room.

'But he can be extremely difficult where women are concerned.'

'Babs, I'm perfectly aware of his reputation.'

'I wasn't necessarily referring to his allegedly lousy behaviour towards women,' retorted Babs. 'It's just that I've seen the other side of the picture—the way women subject him to every bit of adulation as they do the male stars in his films.'

'My heart bleeds for the poor man,' retorted Tessa waspishly.

'Tess, that's not fair! He's a director, not a film star, and he plainly loathes the way those women slaver over him. Not that I'm saying that's quite what you did when he came into the lounge, but he didn't take too kindly to your being so obviously bowled over by him.'

'I wasn't in the least bowled over by him!' exclaimed Tessa indignantly. 'He's simply the first real celebrity I've ever met and I was a bit—well, overawed,' she added lamely. 'I—oh, what's the use?' She opened the door of her room, grabbed her cousin by the arm and pulled her inside.

'Tess, I want to go and have a shower,' protested Babs.

'Just sit down—there's something I want to show you,' muttered Tessa, opening one of the dressing-table drawers and taking out a file. 'You're going to hate me for this,' she muttered, handing her cousin the file.

Babs sat down on the bed, her face expressionless as she glanced through the couple of pages of notes, then turned to the pocket at the back of the file and removed a wodge of press cuttings.

'Who put you up to this, Tess?' she asked quietly.

'I was talking to Ray Linton a couple of months ago— asking him for a job, actually. He mentioned the names of some celebrities and said that if I could come up with a profile on someone of that calibre he'd be prepared to look at my work. Sandro Lambert was one of those names, so when you mentioned helping you out here...' She shook her head miserably as her words petered out. 'It was despicable of me even to think of using you in such a way.'

'You know the sort of paper Ray Linton edits!' exclaimed Babs harshly. 'Profile, my eye! All he's interested in is muck—the more the better!'

'Babs, you know I wouldn't dream of writing anything like that,' protested Tessa hoarsely.

'Yes, I do,' sighed Babs, tossing aside the file. 'Which is why I'm certain that, even if you succeed in writing up some surreptitious article on Sandro, you haven't a chance in hell of having it printed.'

'Why?' demanded Tessa hotly. 'Because my all-powerful stepfather will make sure I don't?'

'Grow up, Tessa,' sighed Babs, rising. 'You never had any real interest in becoming a journalist until you discovered Charles was so against it. For as long as anyone can remember, all you ever wanted was to be a nurse. I know how hard it was on you having to give it up and how difficult it must be having to think in terms of a different career—but are you really certain that journalism is that career?' She walked over to Tessa and gave her an affectionate hug. 'I'm off to pack and have a shower,' she said. 'I'll see you for supper... Oh, yes, and I'll let you have that book I was telling you about— I've finished it.'

Tessa flopped down on to the bed once the door had closed behind Babs, gazing dejectedly around the beautiful, wood-panelled room that had earlier so enchanted her. The thought of her own duplicity had racked her with guilt, she admitted to herself, but, even having confessed, she didn't feel any better. Babs was right—right about everything! Her only ambition had been to become a nurse, and she had sailed through her written exams and had high hopes of doing the same in her practical training until the antiseptics she was coming into increasing contact with had triggered off an allergic reaction in her hands. And Babs was right about her having ogled Sandro Lambert! It was round about the time that her unfortunate tendency towards allergy had manifested itself that so too had her equally unfortunate tendency towards being attracted to completely the wrong sort of man. After the first two—lame, but dauntingly tenacious ducks—it was those dangerously attractive and often virtually unattainable men on whom she had invariably set her sights. Men like Sandro Lambert, she thought with a sudden prickle of apprehension...well, not *exactly* like him, she corrected herself as it occurred to her that she had never in her life met a man with the presence, the almost palpable animal magnetism that this man possessed.

She gave an exasperated shake of her head. There was only one word to describe a woman who could feel as strongly attracted as she had towards a man who hadn't even bothered to acknowledge her existence, let alone exchange a civil word with her—and that word was stupid! Yet nothing she had done warranted the way he had behaved, so why on earth should she feel any guilt? If Sandro Lambert was to be her stepping-stone into journalism, she intended stepping without a qualm!

'It's still open,' she called out at the sound of a knock on the door. 'I've been doing some thinking,' she announced as the door opened.

'Is that so?'

The words, and the appearance of Sandro Lambert in the doorway, brought a shriek of horror from her.

'I thought you were Babs!' she accused, leaping from the bed.

'I can't think why,' he murmured, a look of amusement flitting over his otherwise coolly expressionless face. 'There's something I'd like to discuss with you,' he continued. 'I'm in the Donegal suite at the end of the corridor—I use the sitting-room as my office.'

'I'd be useless as a secretary, if that's what you want to discuss,' she called after him as he turned to leave. What on earth was she saying? she asked herself incredulously the instant the words were out—what more could she have possibly asked for, as far as her proposed article was concerned, than to observe him at work from virtually by his side?

'How refreshingly modest of you,' he drawled, 'especially when you haven't the slightest idea what would be required of you.'

She bit back a groan of frustration as the door closed behind him, then hesitated for only the briefest of moments before dragging it open and racing down the corridor after him.

'It's just that I don't know anything about film work,' she excused herself breathlessly when she had caught up with him.

'A point we had already established,' he observed drily, unlocking the door to the suite and holding it open for her with a mocking bow.

She entered the small hallway and on through the doorway before her into the sitting-room, her eyes discounting the clutter littering just about every available surface. It was a beautiful, high-ceilinged room, its exquisite furnishings matching the same high standards she had noticed throughout the hotel.

'It's a lovely place,' she blurted out, the breathlessness in her words betraying her stifling lack of ease. 'The hotel, I mean…and its surroundings.'

'Ireland is a very beautiful country,' he murmured, flashing her a slightly startled look before clearing the debris from one of the chairs and motioning her to be seated. 'Do you know the country?'

'No, this is my first visit,' replied Tessa, her mental state approaching that of a nervous pupil about to be interrogated by the headmaster as she sat down.

'Tell me, Tessa,' he murmured, removing a bundle of papers from the armchair opposite hers before sitting down on it, 'what do you do?'

'Do?' she echoed, suddenly distracted by the memory of pictures she had seen of Leona Carlotti, the extraordinarily beautiful Italian actress who was his mother, and wondering why she hadn't spotted the obvious family resemblance until this very moment.

'Yes—do,' he snapped, then made a visible effort to curb his impatience. 'Babs mentioned your having stepped in to help her out at the last minute—so I take it you're not in the costume design business?'

'No—I was made redundant just after Christmas,' she said, her own reason warning her only a fraction after his angrily tensing jaw had that she hadn't actually answered his question.

'But you can do shorthand and typing,' he stated in tones that revealed how little used he was to curbing his impatience.

Tessa nodded, her jittery state of mind not in the least helped by sudden thoughts of her present love-hate relationship with her infuriating stepfather. It had been Charles who had suggested a secretarial course once she had been forced to abandon nursing, unblushingly hinting that such skills would be invaluable in the journalism in which she had begun showing an interest and to which, even then, he had probably already decided to block her entry.

'Well, as you may have gathered, there won't be nearly as much wardrobe work as originally anticipated,' continued Sandro, hooking one long, denim-clad leg over an arm of the chair and drumming tanned fingers impatiently against the other.

She could almost sympathise with his irritation, she thought wretchedly, knowing how she would have felt if obliged to contend with the monosyllabic half-wit she must appear to be.

'So, you'll have quite a bit of time on your hands,'

he continued, the strain of the unfamiliar control he was exercising over himself grating in his tone.

'I'd be happy to help you in whatever way I can,' Tessa blurted out, marginally succeeding in her battle to get a grip on herself. 'But you'll have to bear in mind my complete ignorance of filming…and all the technical terms associated with it.'

'I'll keep that uppermost in my mind,' he murmured, exasperation, relief and amusement mingling in his tone. 'Perhaps it would help if I gave you a brief summary of the film and explained my reasons for coming here to shoot the finishing touches?'

'Yes—I'm sure it would!' exclaimed Tessa, a little of her customary confidence returning as relief inexplicably flooded her.

He hadn't really got an accent, she decided some time later, when her ears had become more attuned to that attractively husky voice; it was more that he would now and then express himself in a way that wasn't typically English, despite his flawless command of the language. As she listened she found her mind sifting back through the details she had hurriedly researched on his background. Needless to say, it was his famous mother who was most written about in connection with him. His English father, she vaguely remembered, was something to do with international law and appeared to shun publicity. Perhaps it was the fact that he had been brought up in Italy that accounted for those slight, though most appealing irregularities in his use of English.

'We used the studios for the flashbacks to the central character's medieval ancestor,' he was saying. 'We'd virtually completed shooting when I had to come over here for a couple of days in connection with my next film. I stayed in this hotel and it wasn't until I took a walk along the beach that it hit me I'd found something I wasn't even looking for—the exact location in which to place the flashback scenes.'

'What do you mean by "place" them?' asked Tessa, puzzled. 'If you've already filmed it all and have no cast here—'

'I don't need the cast,' he laughed. 'Well, no more than the three Irish stage actors I'm using. What I want is to capture the brooding magnificence of a landscape virtually untouched by time and link it in with what we've put together in the studio.' The unguarded look on Tessa's face brought an almost teasing smile to his lips. 'You didn't think that what comes up on the screen is filmed in step by step sequence, did you?'

'Of course not,' she muttered, while a panic-stricken voice from within demanded to know how she expected to compile a clandestine, professionally detached appraisal of the working habits of a man whose voice brought her out in goose-bumps and whose smile had the power to turn her legs to jelly. 'It's a shame you won't be able to do all you wanted to,' she said, striving to sound relaxed.

'What do you mean?'

'All those costumes that Babs had sent over—you're not using them now.'

'There's a wedding banquet in one of the flashback scenes. I had considered using the townspeople as extras to depict the contrasting poverty between the guests and the medieval villagers, but I've decided against it.'

'You mean this ghastly flu epidemic has decided for you,' countered Tessa, relieved to hear herself at long last beginning to sound relatively normal.

'No—I mean that I have decided against it,' he informed her coolly, swinging his leg from over the side of the chair and rising with a languid grace to his feet. 'Once I make up my mind I want something, I get it— that's the way I operate.' For all the honeyed warmth of their colour, there was a coolness to match his tone in the eyes that gazed down at her. 'I would suggest you retire early tonight—we get started before dawn.'

Only the thought of what she stood to gain preventing her from giving vent to her fury and telling him what he could do with his wretched job, Tessa leapt to her feet.

'Right, I'll be there!' she flung at him, the fact that she hadn't the slightest idea where 'there' was not even occurring to her in her haste to escape.

Her eyes, now almost navy with the anger seething within her, were trained solely on the doorway through which she would soon mercifully pass, which was why she failed to spot the pile of papers he had earlier tossed on the floor and which now sent her catapulting towards him as her foot skidded across them.

His move to catch her was purely reflex, his tall body hurling itself forward at a precarious angle as his arms reached for her.

Having to force her body forward against the momentum of his to prevent them both from toppling over, Tessa clung on to him for dear life, one arm hooking round his neck while the other clutched at his shoulder.

'Very clumsy,' he drawled, his arms holding her against him like steel clamps while his body set about regaining its balance.

'You're the idiot who littered the floor so dangerously!' she accused indignantly.

She was conscious of hearing her own gasped intake of breath as she looked up into that grimly unsmiling yet disturbingly attractive face hovering scant inches above her own. Then her only awareness was of the excitement stirring within her, numbing her mind to shocked disbelief with the stark sensuality of what was awakening in her.

'You surely can't be complaining—not when it presented you with this opportunity to throw yourself into my arms.' He altered his hold on her, his fingers biting painfully into her flesh as he grasped her by her upper arms. 'Well, now that you're in them,' he mocked softly, 'do they live up to your expectations?'

'Expectations?' squeaked Tessa, almost speechless with fury. 'If I *were* in the habit of throwing myself into the arms of complete strangers—which I'm not—I most certainly wouldn't have picked on an ill-mannered, swollen-headed, arrogant—'

His mouth silenced the remainder of her tirade and, seconds later, shock was the only excuse her stunned mind could come up with for the ease with which his lips had managed to prise open her own and then coax them into what could only be described as enthusiastic participation in the most disturbingly arousing of kisses she had ever experienced.

The detached manner in which her mind was making no attempt whatever to monitor her actions only struck her as alarming when, with no recollection of when or how it had happened, she discovered her head to be cupped in large, deceptively gentle hands and her freed arms wrapped tenaciously around his body.

'No!' she howled, tearing herself free and scrubbing

angrily with the back of her hand against her wildly throbbing mouth.

'Play with fire and you're bound to get burned,' he intoned mockingly. 'Though, I warn you, it will be more than your fingers you'll get burned if you tangle with me. I could tell you I'm off women at the moment—which I am. I could also tell you that you're far too young—which you are. And, more to the point, I could tell you that you're not my type—which you most definitely are not.' His hand snaked out and grasped her by the wrist as she made to turn and run. 'I hope you're taking all this in, Tessa,' he warned with soft menace. 'Because, despite all those things I could tell you, I have—as I'm sure you've heard—an insatiable appetite for women...and I just might decide to amuse myself at your expense.'

CHAPTER TWO

'JUST stay close by me and if there's anything I need you to do I'll let you know,' said Sandro as Tessa stumbled after him down the winding path to the beach in the virtual dark of the bitterly cold morning.

To think that she had spent half the night tossing in sleepless dread of this encounter, she marvelled disgruntledly, whereas he obviously hadn't lost any sleep over what had happened between them on their last meeting.

She had been relieved when he hadn't appeared for dinner the previous evening, but had soon noticed that someone else was also missing.

'That woman we saw earlier—isn't she staying here?' she had enquired of Babs.

'You mean Angelica Bellini,' her cousin had replied with a grin. 'And what you're really asking me is where are she and Sandro.'

'No, I'm—'

'And, given what you're up to,' Babs had continued relentlessly, plainly enjoying herself, 'that's not the sort of question I'm prepared to answer.'

'You know perfectly well my intention is to do a serious article on his professional habits, not something salacious on his love life.'

'What, in the hope that Ray Linton will print it?' Babs had chortled. 'Who do you think you're kidding?'

There was no sense to be had from Babs when she

was in that irritatingly flippant frame of mind, so she had let the subject drop. But her cousin's teasingly exaggerated secrecy had left her with the impression that the director could well be romantically involved with the elusive Angelica, which, if true, and given his earlier behaviour, indicated that he more than deserved his infamy as a womaniser.

'Are you sure you'll be warm enough dressed like that?' asked Sandro, eyeing her slim, jeans-clad legs when he turned and waited while she negotiated the last of the rock-hewn steps on a particularly steep and twisting section of the path.

'Quite sure... Good heavens!' she gasped as the beach below came into sight—a beach that was a hive of industry, littered with men and equipment of every shape and size and bathed in the illusion of bright sunlight by a blinding array of arc lamps. 'I'm not sure what I expected,' she whispered dazedly.

'But nothing like this,' he laughed, the indulgence in his tone surprising her almost as much as the sight below. 'Come on, let's get you down there and introduced to the grim realities of producing fantasy.'

It was only the bitter cold of the January morning that brought any grimness to the proceedings, she had decided a couple of hours later when, chilled to the marrow, she was taking a mental inventory of the meagre wardrobe she had brought with her. The only answer she could think of, to prevent a repeat of the physical agonies she was experiencing, was to wear everything she had brought in layers next time. But not even the piercing bitterness of the wind, nor the fitful drizzle of rain, could detract from her feelings of exhilaration. She was utterly absorbed in what was going on around her, fascinated beyond her every expectation—even though all she was doing, she realised, was watching them line up the shots they planned taking of the incomparably beautiful scenery.

'I'm sure you must be finding all this rather boring,' Sandro called, his broad shoulders hunching against a sudden scurry of wind as he strode back up the beach towards her. 'But you'll soon get the hang of what's going on.'

Tessa smiled and shook her head as he reached her. 'Of course I'm not bored,' she protested, then felt her heart skip several beats. The wind dancing through the inky darkness of his uncovered hair lent an air of almost piratical raffishness to the already dramatically exotic figure he cut. 'I'm finding it all fascinating,' she added unsteadily, thrown by the overwhelming impact he was suddenly having on her.

'But we're not doing anything,' he laughed with a flash of faultlessly formed white teeth. 'We're—' He broke off, the laughter dying to grimness on his face. 'Why are you looking at me like that?' he demanded icily.

'I—I'm sorry,' she stammered, colour flooding her cheeks. 'It's just that I was thinking how like a pirate you looked, walking up the beach—not that I have much idea what a real pirate would look like.'

'A pirate?' he enquired, the grimness fading from him. 'A pirate in designer ski-wear?'

'I'm sorry—it was rude of me,' muttered Tessa, limp with embarrassment and feeling only marginally relieved that he had accepted her outlandish excuse for so openly gawping at him.

'You don't have to be sorry,' he laughed. 'Paolo will

love that; he's convinced pirates must have operated from here in the olden days—' He broke off and bellowed something in Italian to the man standing behind a camera on the shoreline, receiving only an impatiently dismissive wave of the hand in reply.

'When I say we're doing nothing,' Sandro chuckled, 'that's not quite accurate. What's happening is that Paolo's artistic temperament is being indulged.' He smiled as Tessa cast a bemused look in the direction of the cameraman. 'There's something ticking away in his head as he's shooting the bay right now. I've little idea what it is, but I've told him to get on with it anyway.'

'But...' began Tessa, then thought better of it.

'But what?'

'It's just that I thought a director—well, directed, and that everyone else carried out his instructions.'

'That's how it is, for the most part,' he replied easily. 'But I'm not given to playing God with crews the calibre of mine. When a man of Paolo's genius behind the camera has a hunch, it's more often than not an inspired hunch—I'd be a fool not to indulge him.'

Tessa was mentally nodding as she returned her gaze to the camera. Almost the first thing she had noticed was the atmosphere of relaxed camaraderie in which so many different nationalities interacted. But the apparent effortlessness of such interaction was, she now realised, due to the taut professionalism of the highly skilled men involved and their obvious respect and affection for the man whose creative genius co-ordinated their skills.

'Do you always work with the same crew?' she asked.

'I tend to pick my crews from a fairly narrow circle,' he replied. 'Unfortunately there are times when lack of availability forces me to compromise—though where cinematographers are concerned, if Paolo or a guy by the name of Umberto Bellini wasn't available, I'd probably choose to wait till one or the other was.'

'Umberto Bellini—wasn't he the man hurt in an accident on one of your films?'

'Yes,' he muttered. 'Poor Umberto—' He broke off, a guarded expression coming to his face before, to her complete bewilderment, he began speaking in Italian.

It was only when she realised he must be addressing someone else that Tessa turned round, appalled awareness flitting unguardedly through her mind of how ghastly she must look as she saw approaching the tall figure of the woman she had fleetingly glimpsed the previous day.

'Have you two met?' asked Sandro, a discernible edge to his tone as he switched back to English.

'No, we haven't,' said the woman, her smile accentuating the striking beauty of her face as she removed a gloved hand from beneath the elegant tartan wrap draped around her. 'It's so good to find another woman here,' she murmured in perfect, slightly American-accented English as she shook hands with Tessa. 'You must be about the only female crew member not to have succumbed to this dreadful flu.'

'Tessa isn't a member of the crew, she's just kindly agreed to fill in for Carla,' said Sandro before Tessa had a chance to speak. His mouth tightened to a grim line when Angelica made a teasing-sounding comment to him in Italian. 'I don't think Tessa speaks Italian,' he stated with brusque pointedness.

'Oh, I am sorry!' exclaimed Angelica, placing a placating hand on the sleeve of Tessa's rain-soaked anorak. 'That was terribly rude of me.'

'Not at all—' began Tessa, only to be cut off by Sandro.

'Tessa was just enquiring after Umberto,' he said. 'Did you manage to get through to him last night?'

'I did, and I've lots of messages for you from him— but I can tell you all that later,' replied Angelica, then turned to Tessa. 'You're one of the few friends of my brother's I haven't met.'

'Oh, I don't know him!' exclaimed Tessa. 'It's just that my cousin told me about the accident he had. I do hope he's better.'

'He's recovering nicely,' murmured the woman, her eyes returning once more to the man beside them. 'Darling, isn't it time you had a break? You look frozen,' she chided softly.

'I'm fine,' he stated abruptly, then glanced at Tessa who was attempting to distract herself by trying to re-member what it was like to have feeling in her legs. 'But you're not—are you, little one?' He took her gently by the shoulder and turned her to face him, frowning as he examined her bedraggled appearance. 'I think it's about time you returned to the hotel and got yourself thawed out. I shan't be needing you this afternoon; I've a meet-ing lined up with the actors we're using.'

'But I'm fine—honestly,' protested Tessa, not in the least happy with the idea of being given special treat-ment. 'There's no reason why I shouldn't stay on till the rest of you have finished.'

'I've just given you a reason,' snapped Sandro, 'so do as you're told.'

Annoyed by his tone, Tessa was about to make an angry retort when it suddenly hit her how obtuse she was being. Special treatment didn't come into it—he wanted her out of the way now that Angelica had arrived, and she had been too stupid to take the hint.

'I...well, this afternoon I'll go into town and get some notepads and pencils,' she muttered lamely, then turned to Angelica. 'It was nice meeting you.'

'We'll be running into one another all the time now,' smiled Angelica. 'We could have tea later.'

Still smarting from her own stupidity and ignoring the protests coming from her numbed limbs, Tessa changed her mind about going straight back to the hotel and made her way along the beach towards the town.

Only the day before, her first sight of the small town of Rathmullan, nestling sleepily on the shores of Lough Swilly with its magnificent backdrop of heather-hued mountains, had taken her breath away and filled her with an inexpressible joy. Today, feeling miserable and confused as she did, the mist-laden beauty of her surroundings only served to make her feel worse.

There wasn't anything wrong with what she was doing, she argued with herself; if someone in the public eye chose not to co-operate with the Press, it was common knowledge that slightly underhand methods were often used to satisfy the public's interest. And by interest she didn't mean scurrilous curiosity about his private life, she meant the sort of balanced article she intended compiling on his professional life. All right, so she wasn't yet a bona fide journalist, but she had to start somewhere!

She entered one of the shops in a terrace of small, stone-fronted cottages lining the rain-washed main street and bought notepads, pencils and an English newspaper. Further along she got herself a heavyweight tracksuit that looked as though it might keep her reasonably warm on days as bitterly cold as this particular one.

But as she made her way back to the hotel, along a heavily wooded path running parallel to the shoreline below, she began asking herself why, if she was so sure she was doing nothing wrong, she was still feeling so confused and dejected.

Probably because she still wasn't one hundred per cent convinced she was right, she answered herself gloomily. Or was she being completely honest with herself? Because she might as well face up to it that, true to form, she was yet again attracted to a man who was completely unsuitable—though unsuitable was hardly the word, she informed herself grimly. Sandro Lambert wasn't unsuitable in the relatively mundane way one or two other men had been. This time she was way out of her depth; up against a man who not only had looks that many a woman would be reduced to drooling over, but who was also an international celebrity—the sort of man who had women such as the stunning Angelica Bellini virtually at his beck and call!

She felt shame burn through her when she remembered how her juvenile gawping had irritated him. And the only reason he had kissed her was because, as he had so quickly pointed out, she had flung herself into his arms—the fact that she had done so accidentally being neither here nor there.

She walked through the grounds of the hotel, darting round to the back entrance when she saw Sandro in a group of men emerging from the path leading from the beach…he was the last person she felt like facing at that moment.

She was behaving like a lunatic, she remonstrated an-

grily with herself when she reached her room and began
shedding her damp clothing. Spending half the night
agonising over the fact that a man she barely knew had
kissed her was bad enough; becoming reduced to sneak-
ing round corners to avoid that same man was downright
lunacy!

She kept her mind occupied by running over Babs's
wardrobe instructions as she took a long, hot bath and
then washed her hair. Later, her hair wrapped in a towel
and her body in a snowy white bathrobe, she flopped
down on the bed and began glancing through the newspaper she had bought earlier. In its centre pages she
came across a light-heartedly written article entitled 'Unfaithful Heart-Throbs Given their Marching Orders'. The
subject matter—women who had broken off their en-
gagements to straying famous men—was of no particular
interest to her. It was the apparently effortless, almost
throw-away style of the writing that caught her attention
and thoroughly depressed her as she realised just how
limited her own writing skills were by comparison. It
was only at the very end of the article, in a list citing a
number of other men in the public eye whose fiancées
had abandoned them because of their constant woman-
ising, that she spotted a familiar name.

Rising from the bed, she flung aside the paper and
went over to the dressing-table. So Sandro had been engaged to a childhood sweetheart who had decided
enough was enough only a few weeks ago, she thought
as she switched on the drier and began drying her hair—
so what? It was all no doubt covered in those articles on
him she had hastily got together before leaving London
but hadn't yet found time to read, she told herself, then
gave her entire attention to the drying of her hair when

it crossed her mind that she had had plenty of time to read them, including last night...or even right now.

She switched off the drier and was vigorously brushing her gleaming, shoulder-length hair when a tap on the door made her turn.

The door was half-open and Sandro was lounging against its frame with the air of one who had been doing so for some time.

'I knocked a couple of times, but you probably couldn't hear me over the noise of your hairdrier,' he said, closing the door behind him and strolling over to where she sat at the dressing-table. 'You've missed lunch,' he informed her, stooping to pick up the tortoiseshell-backed brush that had slipped from her hand and placing it on the dressing-table top.

'I'm not hungry.'

'But you couldn't have had much in the way of breakfast either.'

'I'll eat tonight,' she muttered, tensing with consternation at the sudden pounding of her heart.

'Why did you go tearing off into town instead of back to the hotel earlier?'

'Because I—' She broke off, furious to find herself actually embarking on answering him. 'What business is it of yours? Anyone would think you were my father— going on about my skipping meals and not doing as I'm told!'

He leaned over and took her chin in his hand, forcing her to meet his gaze.

'That's probably because I'm not sure whether you're twelve or twenty,' he replied, both his voice and face confusingly devoid of expression.

'Which age did you think I was last night?' she demanded angrily as she twisted free from his hold, and could have bitten off her tongue as soon as she'd said it.

'I didn't expect you to take my words quite that literally,' he informed her in drawling tones, his eyes glowering down into hers. 'What age are you, anyway?'

'Why should my age be of any concern to you?' she demanded before she had time to think better of it.

'You answer my question first—then I'll answer yours,' he mocked, a half-smile flickering across his lips while the scowling darkness remained unaltered in his eyes.

'Twenty-three.'

'Yes—I think I can accept that,' he murmured, 'now that you're not sporting your usual infantile hairstyle.' As he spoke he casually reached out and ran his fingers through the silky luxuriance of her hair.

Tessa wondered, as she drew her head sharply back from the electrifying touch of those trespassing fingers, if there was any way he could have sensed the magnitude of the effect they had had on her, and felt a shiver of horror ripple through her at the very idea.

'I...weren't you supposed to answer my question...now that I've answered yours?' she gabbled, then realised she hadn't the faintest idea what that question was.

'Why should your age be any concern of mine?' he mused, mercifully jogging her traumatised memory. 'Perhaps women do mature much younger than men, but at thirty-one I do really feel I'm a bit old to be getting involved with teenagers.'

It was on the tip of Tessa's tongue to ask exactly what

he meant by 'involved'; she felt slightly giddy with relief when she succeeded in biting back the words.

'I'm glad you understand what I mean,' he murmured.

'I'm surprised to hear that, considering I know *exactly* what you mean!' exploded Tessa, all thought of caution deserting her. 'Which, to quote you, is that, despite my most definitely not being your type, you've decided to amuse yourself at my expense!'

'As I've said before, I wish you wouldn't take my remarks quite as literally as you appear to,' he drawled.

'What am I supposed to do—search your bald utterances for some subtly hidden flattery?' she demanded scathingly.

'Forget what I said yesterday,' he murmured softly, his hands this time reaching out to the lapels of her bathrobe, prising them slowly apart before sliding his hands up to cup the shoulders he had exposed.

Tessa's own hands rose agitatedly, not in any attempt to remove his, but to clutch her gaping robe over her breasts.

'But you're entitled to be flattered by how strongly attracted I am to the strange mixture I find in you of innocence and—' He broke off, drawing her sharply to her feet.

'Of innocence and what?' she croaked, unable to stop herself.

'You have to understand that English isn't my first language,' he whispered, his words baffling her while the glow softening his eyes held her in mesmerised thrall. 'I express myself far better, in times like these, in Italian.'

His arms had encircled her and his mouth was coaxing open hers before she had even begun querying the sense of his words. She became vaguely aware of her hands, still clutching at her robe and now trapped between their bodies, but there was no way her stunned mind could distinguish whether the violent pounding of heartbeats against them was a product of one heart or two.

There had been men who had managed to stir an awareness in her of the powerful potential of her own latent desire, but it was only in this man's arms that a once-shadowy awareness erupted into a violent awakening. And it wasn't simply the sensuous sweetness of the mouth taking such burning advantage of the eager acquiescence of hers that was threatening to demolish the control she had never before had need to exercise, it seemed to be everything about him—the slight graze of his incipient beard against her skin; the aura of explosive virility emanating from that lean, hard body entrapping her own; that hint of fragrance, subtle yet unquestionably masculine, a scent that was exclusively his. For the first time in her life she knew herself to be in the arms of a man capable of stripping her bare of every defence she possessed...and her only reaction was her body's eager participation in the wonder of its erotic awakening.

'Hell, Tessa,' he groaned, tearing his mouth from its passionate exploration of hers and burying his face against her hair, 'I'm supposed to be meeting those actors this afternoon, not whiling it away making love to you.' He lowered his head, his mouth searching hotly in the curve of her neck while his hands moved impatiently to the knotted belt of her robe.

By making love, her sluggish mind began warning her, this man meant a good deal more than a passionate exchange of kisses.

'Shall I put them off till this evening?' he breathed

huskily. 'Then we'll be free to spend the afternoon making love and, in between, getting to know one another.'

He couldn't have expressed it any plainer than that, shrieked out her now almost fully restored mind— and this, remember, was the same man who had so arrogantly informed her that, despite her many shortcomings, he might just decide to amuse himself at her expense!

'I see you've made up your mind,' she stated, her voice tight with strain.

He responded instantly to what he must have detected in her tone, his head rising as his arms released her.

'Made up my mind?'

'Yes—to amuse yourself at my expense.'

'Wouldn't it have been a mutual amusement?' he enquired, the softness of passion in his eyes giving way to the sharpness of ice.

'For your information, I go in for slightly more conventional ways of getting to know men than leaping into bed with them,' she informed him icily, moving hurriedly away from him.

'That didn't exactly answer my question,' he drawled. 'And, for *your* information, there's no need for you to put all that space between us; I'm not given to forcing my attentions on women…not that it would be necessary with you.'

'I beg your pardon?' exclaimed Tessa, trembling with rage.

'Grow up, Tessa,' he snapped. 'I'm experienced enough to know when I've a responsive woman in my arms—no matter how much she chooses to protest once she's safely out of them.'

'Well, I wouldn't let that go to your head if I were

you,' she flung at him angrily. 'Not with the sort of louse I'm invariably attracted to!'

'I'd love to stay and continue this delightful conversation, darling,' he drawled, strolling to the door, 'but I've those actors to meet.'

So cool, so completely distanced from the man whose passion had turned her world upside-down only moments before, she thought with numbed bemusement as the door closed behind him. Only the most practised of seducers could have put on a display so calculatedly convincing...and only the most naïve of fools would have been so thoroughly taken in—and then compounded her stupidity by making herself sound little better than a gangster's moll in her attempts to excuse herself.

CHAPTER THREE

TESSA huddled her slim body against a sand dune as another gust of wind scudded ferociously across the beach. *I wish the film crew would stop fiddling around and get on with things,* she thought miserably, feeling frozen and redundant. She liked to be fully occupied, not left alone and at the mercy of thoughts that would inevitably leave her feeling even more confused and alienated.

Absorbing and exhausting, it was these long hours of work that normally proved her salvation—a shelter into which she could retreat and leave behind the perplexities of a world in which she no longer felt secure. There were even times, when she hadn't her work to distract her, when she felt pangs of acute homesickness—when she longed for her mother's gentle humour, the noisy presence of her half-brother, Rupert, and perhaps most of all those long, chatty walks she and her stepfather used to take before her journalistic ambitions had thrown up that invisible barrier between them.

Charles would love it here, she thought wistfully as she gazed down the beach, her eyes dulling with resentment as they came to rest on the tall, slim figure that stood out from the rest. Sandro, too, became another person when at work, she thought, frowning as she found herself having to make a conscious effort not to allow her gaze to linger. There were times when he became oblivious of the fact that it was no longer the paragon

Carla he had at his beck and call, but she didn't really mind that; it was those times when he would forget and call her Carla that she most often felt the closest she ever came to being at ease with him. But outside the safe confines of work he reduced her to a mass of confusion.

He was using her, she told herself bitterly, though she had no idea why. And Angelica—why did she have this unpleasant feeling that Angelica was using her too? Never in a million years would she feel at ease with Angelica…yet Angelica constantly sought her company.

She gave a small shudder as she remembered the feelings that had assailed her that terrible afternoon when, not long after Sandro had left to meet the Irish actors, she had answered the knock on her door and found Angelica standing there. Not once during those moments of madness in Sandro's arms had any thought of the beautiful Italian woman entered her mind, yet surely not even an out-and-out adulteress could have felt any more guilty and hopeless than she had on opening the door that afternoon.

About the only thing they could claim to have in common was the fact that they were the only two women staying at the hotel, thought Tessa with a sigh, yet whenever she had a free moment there was Angelica at her side…and letting her know, without ever actually uttering a word on the subject, that Sandro was hers and hers alone, no matter what appearances might indicate to the contrary. And what, exactly, did appearances indicate? She hadn't a clue, she realised with a defeated shake of her head before casting an anxious look along the beach and praying they would start the work in which she could become involved.

Only a woman of supreme confidence could react with the serene lack of concern Angelica always displayed during those ghastly times when Sandro would so blatantly flirt with the only other female guest present. He could easily have picked on one of the maids, thought Tessa angrily, but no, he had to pick on her! And even Paolo had objected: though she didn't speak a word of Italian, she had instinctively known that that was what Paolo had been remonstrating with him over in the bar the other night. But, unlike herself, Paolo obviously knew the true nature of Sandro's relationship with Angelica and whatever it was about it that resulted in another woman being used as an unwitting pawn. And that was exactly how she was being used, she told herself with a shudder of resentment, wondering how it was that she hadn't instantly sensed those dark currents of intensity pulsating back and forth between the almost detachedly serene Italian woman and the brooding, often volatile director.

If this were a film scenario, she told herself bitterly, Angelica and Sandro would be the stars…and she a bit player plucked for use from the crowd.

'Tessa!' Sandro bellowed over to her. 'Take the yellow mark against the rocks and let Paolo line up on you!'

Like one offered a reprieve, Tessa leapt up, digging in her pocket for her notepad as she raced over to the rocks.

'It's quite simple, really,' he had told her on one of those rare occasions when he had remembered his promise to make allowances for her ignorance and had explained a procedure to her—instead of leaving her to pump a crew member as she usually did. 'Some directors use markers to guide every step of every scene, but I don't—I feel it inhibits the natural flow of an actor's movements. But the three we're using aren't experienced in film work, and as we're short on rehearsal time I'm afraid we'll have to do quite a bit of choreography. In the studio each actor would be allocated his own colour, and the continuity people would then chalk the movements out in the relevant colours. Obviously chalk won't be any good on wet sand, so we'll have to come up with something else.'

Her hands trembling from the bitter cold, Tessa leafed through her pad till she found what she wanted. Using her notes as a guide to where she had placed the wads of Plasticine she had decided on as a substitute for chalk, she let her eyes scan the rocks. Suppressing a slight twinge of alarm when she found nothing, she looked again at her notes. Just the three single markers were involved in this particular scene, she thought frustratedly, one yellow for the father, one red and one blue for each of the sons—they didn't even have to move, just remain immobile as they gazed out to sea. So simple, she told herself wryly as she felt the stirrings of panic, but it had taken what had seemed like interminable hours of agonising for Sandro and Paolo to work out precisely where each man was to be positioned!

'Tessa!'

'Hang on a minute!' she yelled back, trying desperately to calm herself as she started scanning the rocks further along for the blue marker…the red marker…any marker!

'For God's sake, just position yourself in front of that large rock to the left of you!' roared Sandro. 'To your *left*!' he bellowed when she hesitated a fraction.

Now completely unnerved, Tessa tripped over a piece

of half-buried rock and almost went sprawling in her rush to carry out the orders now coming fast and furious from a plainly irate director.

Thoughts of her article had somehow slipped to the back of her mind in the past few days, but one of these days she would produce the definitive article on dictatorial directors, she vowed vengefully to herself as she shivered in the icy wind, not daring to move a muscle while Sandro and Paolo fussed around, jabbering away to one another in Italian and seeking, in their usual, mind-bogglingly pernickety manner, the correct angle for this, the perfect approach shot for that... But she would probably be accused of gross exaggeration, she thought peevishly. For example, anyone witnessing this particular instance of artistic agonising between director and cinematographer would automatically assume that the most crucial scene in the entire film was about to be shot—they would never believe that this was merely a discussion on a few options for tomorrow's shoot!

'Right, we're calling it a day,' Sandro bawled over to her, after what had seemed like hours and during which the rain had begun drizzling down and seeping its way through her clothing to chill the few parts of her that the wind hadn't already turned to blocks of ice.

'I'll be up in a minute,' she called back, only now noticing that the crew, and most of the equipment, had already disappeared from the beach. 'There's just something I want to check.'

'What, exactly, is it you want to check?' demanded Sandro from behind her a few moments later.

Tessa, pretending not to have heard, continued consulting her now rain-splattered notes.

'I thought I suggested using paint for the markers,' he

said, his eyes narrowing with impatience as they scanned the mark-free line of rocks.

Tessa bit back an indignant retort. He had made a number of suggestions, but had left her with the impression that he was leaving the ultimate decision to her.

'I didn't think you'd want us to be accused of defacing a place of such beauty—which is what we'd be doing using paint, as anything other than permanent wouldn't survive the weather,' she informed him as calmly as she was able. 'So I decided to use Plasticine.'

'So where is this Plasticine you decided to use?' he enquired, patience personified.

'I don't know,' she muttered, turning to offer him her apologies and feeling fury blaze in her as she met an expression she could only describe as one of mockery. 'And you know perfectly well I don't! It must have come off!'

'Of course it's come off,' he retorted cuttingly. 'This isn't the Mediterranean, in case you hadn't noticed. These rocks are submerged every time the tide comes in. Surely even you wouldn't expect daubs of Plasticine to survive that!'

'Moron that I am, I did!' exploded Tessa. 'So just go away and leave me in peace to work out where I put them,' she pleaded, once more burying her nose in her notepad.

She didn't even bother attempting resistance when she felt the pad being removed from her frozen hands. She stood there in bristling silence as he leafed unhurriedly through its pages, plotting how she would set about converting her experiences of the past few days into an article that would impress Ray Linton, because one thing was certain—she had had all the experience she was ever likely to get of observing Sandro Lambert at work.

'Come on,' he said, handing her back the notepad; 'let's get back to the hotel before we both drown.' He gave a sudden shake of his soaked head, then grinned as rivulets of rain cascaded down his face.

'But what about the markers?' croaked Tessa, her mind unable to adjust to the fact that she appeared not to have been fired.

'What about them?' he shrugged. 'Anything we try using now is bound to be washed off by the morning—even quick-drying paint would have no hope of drying in this sort of weather. We'll leave it till the morning and, with the aid of your most excellent notes, mark it out with Plasticine.'

Laughter began rumbling in his throat at the sight of Tessa's bemused disbelief. 'Tessa, you really...oh, hell—no!' he groaned as the heavens opened up and began tipping their all down on them. 'Quick—the old boat-house,' he ordered, grabbing her by the arm and leading her up the sands to the dilapidated entrance of the boat-house which the grips had once considered as a temporary equipment store and rejected once they had looked it over.

Inside it was simply a huge cave, its rocky surfaces hewn smooth in a bygone age. At one stage massive iron and wood gates had been erected across the entrance which, over the years, had become reduced to huge piles of beam-sized planks of wood and rusting iron rubble that barred safe access to the back of the cave.

'At least we'll be out of the rain in here,' announced Sandro, climbing nimbly over a pile of wood and seating himself on one of the beams.

Tessa made no comment as she stood huddled as close to the entrance as she could without the torrenting rain blowing in on her. Not that a few drops more would make any difference, she thought with a shiver—her new tracksuit offered only reasonable protection from the wind, but none from the rain, and her legs were now soaked to the skin.

'Aren't you coming up to join me?' he called.

'I'm fine here,' she replied, praying that the downpour would end as quickly as it had started and racking her brains for something to say that was work-related. If she had to be alone with him she would far rather it was with the director preoccupied by his work than with that other man she found herself both repelled and attracted by.

'OK—I'll come down and join you.'

Tessa spun round in alarm at the clattering sounds coming from behind her and was just in time to see him land on his feet beside her.

'You're soaked!' he exclaimed, his eyes sweeping over her bedraggled figure. 'Perhaps I should lend you one of these—they're ideal for this climate,' he added, grinning as he indicated his ski-suit, one of an apparently endless supply he possessed. 'Though it would probably take two of you to fill anything that fits me,' he murmured, his eyes making a more leisurely inspection of her.

Feeling tense and on edge, Tessa returned to gazing out at the rain without saying a word.

'Oh, dear—I really am in your bad books.' He sighed mockingly. 'Come on—let's make friends.' As he spoke he reached out a hand to her, a startled look flickering across his face when she punched his hand aside with a tightly clenched fist.

'My, what's happened to the girl who couldn't keep her eyes off me?' he mocked. 'And here I am, just trying to be friendly.'

'You're the last person I'd want as a friend!' she lashed out.

'What do you want me as, Tessa?' he drawled. 'A lover?'

'Just who the hell do you think you are?' she demanded, almost beside herself with fury. 'You think you—'

'If there's one thing I can't stand, it's others taking it upon themselves to tell me what they imagine I'm thinking,' he cut in icily. 'It irritates me almost as much as it does when women I've never met before and in whom I've not the slightest interest start behaving as though they'd never seen a man before. Women like that shouldn't be surprised when I retaliate and they find their stupidity backfiring on them.'

'Backfiring on them?' croaked Tessa, stunned by the savagery in his words. 'You're unbalanced!'

'I could well be,' he drawled, 'but you're hardly in a position to judge.'

'Am I not?' she asked numbly. 'Do you think I'm too stupid not to realise when I'm being used? You've already started extracting the price you've decided I'm to pay for having had the temerity to look at you in a way men regard as their God-given right when they're the ones doing the looking—but, whatever this game is that you and Angelica are playing, nothing gives you the right to involve me in it!'

'Game?' he demanded harshly. 'You think Angelica and I are playing a game?'

'I've had enough!' Tessa rounded on him angrily. 'People like you are completely beyond my comprehension!'

She stormed off out into the rain, raising her face in welcome to its harshly invigorating sting.

'Who are people like me, Tessa?'

The sound of his voice had come from right behind her, but she kept on walking.

'OK, if you won't answer that, perhaps you'll answer this,' he persisted, overtaking her, then mocking her with his laughter as he turned and began walking backwards in front of her. 'Why are you so afraid of being alone with me?'

Tessa glared at him as she halted rather than walk straight into him. 'Go away and amuse yourself at someone else's expense—just leave me alone!'

'Poor Tessa, it still rankles, doesn't it?' he mocked. 'But are you absolutely certain that you really do want me to leave you alone?' He laughed, lunging forward to catch her and then twirling her giddily in his arms.

The ferocity with which she lashed out and freed herself left her trembling with shock and there were tears mingling with the rain streaming down her face as she raced to the path, slipping and sliding her way up its now treacherous surface towards the sanctuary of the hotel.

She had had to fight him like that, she excused herself with choking bitterness, because, soaked and frozen though she was, the instant his arms had encircled her she had felt on fire. It was humiliating and disgusting and a thousand things more terrible...but all he had to do was touch her and she wanted him.

'Tessa!'

'Oh—hello, Angelica...I'm afraid I'm a bit wet,' she gasped at the woman she had almost run into as she entered the warmth of the foyer.

'You poor dear, you're drenched. I really must speak to Alessandro about the terrible conditions under which—'

'Angelica, I'm dripping all over the place...I'll see you later, but right now I need a bath!'

She raced past the woman and straight up the stairs to her room.

It always threw her when Angelica referred to Sandro by his full name, Alessandro, she thought as, struggling from her clothes, she entered the bathroom and started running a bath. With a bit of luck Alessandro would also have walked slap into Angelica—who could tend the wounds she hoped she had inflicted in plenty on him, she thought as she gingerly flexed the fingers of her throbbing right hand.

Having bathed and dried her hair, she found she felt, if anything, even more on edge than she had before. She had always been useless when it came to arguments, she thought miserably; it was usually long after they had finished that the right words would come to her. For heaven's sake, all she had done was give the wretched man a few, perhaps too lingering, appreciative looks when she first saw him—the way he had carried on anyone would have thought she had clambered on to his knee and tried to strip him! If he thought a lingering look warranted retribution, how on earth would he react to the article she intended writing? And write it she would, she vowed vehemently, and tout it around to every newspaper in Christendom if Ray Linton didn't want it!

She was just about to dig out her file when a knock on the door heralded Angelica, accompanied by a maid carrying a tea-tray.

'You looked so miserable, my dear, and as it's a bit early for anything stronger I thought I'd order us some tea,' announced Angelica, who then instructed the maid to leave the tray on the bedside table and drew herself up a chair. 'You stretch yourself out on the bed while I see to this,' she instructed Tessa as she began pouring the tea. 'I think it's time we had a little talk.'

Sandro Lambert wasn't the only topic of conversation in the world, Tessa reminded herself in an effort to calm the frantic beating of her heart as she got up on the bed and wedged the pillows at her back before sitting up against the bed-rest.

'You must forgive Alessandro for the way he's been behaving,' sighed Angelica, destroying any remnant of hope Tessa might have had. 'I keep telling him that if he has to take his anger out on anyone it should be me— not an innocent bystander such as you,' she added, passing Tessa a cup. 'But the poor darling always has been over-protective where I'm concerned and…' She gave a delicate shrug of her slim shoulders. 'Whether Alessandro likes it or not, I feel you are owed an explanation.'

Oh, yes? thought Tessa, her eyes wary as they took in the elegant figure seated by her bed and dressed, as always, stunningly—this time in a coral knitted silk dress that set off her dark beauty to perfection.

'This isn't easy for me,' sighed Angelica. 'I feel as

though I'm breaking the trust of the man I love... Oh, yes,' she murmured with a melting smile as she caught Tessa's startled look. 'The man I love and who, believe it or not, loves me.'

It wasn't so difficult to believe, thought Tessa, as she tried to ignore the sudden gnawing ache in the pit of her stomach.

'The very first time Alessandro and I met...it was the day when something beautiful leapt instantly between us, yet the day, apart from that, we'd rather had never existed.' She leaned back in her chair, the almost trance-like expression on her face making Tessa feel slightly uneasy—but then, she asked herself, when had she ever felt in the least at ease with Angelica?

'I'd been living in the States for several years and on my first day back in Italy all I wanted was to visit my beloved brother Umberto—so I went to the set where he was filming. You already know of the terrible accident to my brother...but that was the day it happened, and I was there to witness it all.'

'How terrible for you!' exclaimed Tessa with genuine horror.

'That Umberto was the only one trapped when the scaffolding collapsed was something of a miracle—there were so many people around. It was also a miracle that Alessandro wasn't killed when he freed him...there were damaged high-voltage cables everywhere and the gaffer, the man in charge of electrics, had been knocked un-conscious by a piece of falling scaffolding.'

'Just how badly was your poor brother hurt?' asked Tessa.

'His legs were horribly crushed—which was what Alessandro had spotted from where he was standing. He told me afterwards that he had had a premonition that Umberto would lose his legs if he didn't act immediately.'

'How terrible,' gasped Tessa. 'Are his legs all right?'

'There was a time when it was thought he'd lose them—now his doctors are talking about his working again one day.'

'Sandro must be very fond of him to have risked his life like that saving him,' said Tessa quietly.

'He is,' replied Angelica, 'but it was knowing I was there that gave him the strength to do what he did.' She gave a softly reminiscent laugh. 'You may not believe this, but once it was all over I found the poor darling being as sick as a dog behind one of the sheds. My big, brave Alessandro,' she sighed, 'yet he was like a little boy in his embarrassment when he confessed to me that he'd always been very squeamish over the sight of blood.'

Tessa took a sip from her cup, feeling a pang of guilt over her cynical reaction to hearing Sandro being described as looking like a small boy—and she was also beginning to wonder where all this was leading.

'It was then that all our troubles started,' said Angelica, almost as though she had heard Tessa's silent query. 'You see, Alessandro blamed himself for what had happened—simply because it took place on one of his sets. And he became irrationally protective towards both Umberto and me—almost superstitiously so—and has continued being so ever since.'

Tessa experienced yet another pang of guilt; she just couldn't stop Sandro's face from leaping vividly to her mind, laughing in disbelieving rejection of the pictures being painted of him.

'It was almost as though he'd decided to punish himself for what had happened by denying himself the comfort our love should have brought him,' continued Angelica. 'How can you put love on hold?' she asked dramatically. 'Because that's what he's attempting to do. Until Umberto is fully recovered, he won't allow himself any open acknowledgement of our love. It's almost as though he's convinced himself that our love is inextricably tied up with my brother's recovery, which could be jeopardised by any deviation from this rigid rule he's set himself.'

'But wasn't Sandro engaged to someone else until quite recently?' asked Tessa, the article she had recently read springing to her mind.

'Oh, Carol!' exclaimed Angelica almost dismissively. 'Yes, he became engaged to her shortly after we met. But, of course, it didn't last—she soon realised how he felt about me.'

'Why on earth did he get engaged to her in the first place?' asked Tessa, unable to mask her shock.

'To keep the Press from having any suspicions about us—though you can imagine how hurt I was until I realised.'

Not half as much as the unfortunate Carol must have been, thought Tessa, hardly able to believe her ears— even though she herself, to a much lesser degree, had been on the receiving end of Sandro and Angelica's propensity for using others.

'Alessandro, as you can imagine, is paranoid at the idea of the Press getting to hear about us—just one careless word is all it would take…which is why he's so beside himself with worry at the moment.'

'I'm sure the staff here can be trusted,' said Tessa,

the somewhat detached thought occurring to her that 'beside himself with worry' was hardly an apt description of Sandro's demeanour today or any other day.

'I can only pray you're right.'

'If that's the case, I'm surprised you came here,' muttered Tessa, then added hastily in a slightly less judgemental tone, 'I mean—knowing how paranoid Sandro is about possible publicity.'

'I was silly, I know,' sighed Angelica. 'But when I heard Carla was ill I dropped everything and came here without thinking, knowing he'd need someone.'

'Oh, you do shorthand and typing, do you?' asked Tessa, unable to hide her surprise.

'No, but we'd have worked something out—I know exactly how his mind works. If only he had let me help him instead of taking you on, we'd have had a ready-made excuse for my presence should the Press find out!' she exclaimed agitatedly. 'But he was so afraid he'd be unable to disguise his real feelings for me in front of the crew—though I'm sure many of them are aware of our true feelings for one another.' She gazed pleadingly at Tessa. 'Tell me you'll forgive his terrible behaviour, Tessa…please. It's only his way of trying to protect our love.' She reached over and patted Tessa on the arm, then rose to her feet. 'I'm afraid I must go now—I'm expecting a call from one of my brother's doctors.'

Apart from closing her eyes, Tessa didn't move a muscle once she heard the door close behind Angelica. If Sandro was a man in love, she'd eat her hat!

She lay there for several seconds, her mind spinning. She simply didn't know what to think! It wasn't that she didn't actually believe Angelica; her every word had carried a solid ring of conviction. OK, she was strongly attracted to Sandro, she admitted with ruthless candour, but she certainly didn't view him through rose-tinted spectacles…yet just about everything Angelica had come out with ran contrary to what she knew of him.

She gave a confused shake of her head. Whatever her instinctive reservations about Angelica's outpourings, even if only half of them were true, Sandro was even more of an unprincipled louse than she could have imagined.

CHAPTER FOUR

'CUT!' roared Sandro, and so loudly that Tessa, standing some distance away from him, nearly leapt out of her skin. He then began reciting words in Italian that brought an eruption of cheers from the crew and a look of bemusement to Tessa's face.

'What's happened?' she asked as he joined her.

'All that's ever going to happen as far as shooting goes on this particular masterpiece.' He grinned. 'That's it—we've finished!'

'So—it's going to be a masterpiece, is it?' teased Tessa, and was immediately conscious of just how relaxed she had sounded...and actually felt.

'An unquestionable masterpiece,' he laughingly assured her. 'Hang on a second while I give those two ruffians a hand!' he exclaimed when two of the grips, a pair of boisterous young clowns for whom Tessa had developed a particularly soft spot, showed signs of having difficulty with the equipment they were dismantling.

She watched as Sandro went to their assistance and afterwards took one of them by the scruff of the neck and threatened to dunk him in the sea.

She gave a sudden, exasperated shake of her head and turned her gaze from the antics of the three men when what had become a disturbingly familiar softness started melting through her. It was just as well this crazy period of topsy-turvy confusion in her life was soon to end, she told herself firmly, but it was a thought tinged with wistfulness and an unsettling sensation of emptiness.

After Angelica's disclosures, she had felt oddly secure in the certainty that the spell she had been under had been irreparably broken...but things hadn't turned out quite as she had expected. Perhaps Angelica had spoken to him, but, whether she had or not, from that day on his attitude towards her had improved markedly. Or perhaps it was simply the fact that they had been working flat out for the past couple of days, she thought with a sigh; even when things had been at their worst he had never let it interfere with their working relationship, which had always been remarkably, almost paradoxically good.

'Those two!' he complained with mock-exasperation when he rejoined her. 'I've told them I'm having them gagged and put in strait-jackets for my next film.'

'When do you start on the next one?'

'The package was put together months ago,' he replied, then smiled at her look of incomprehension. 'That's what the producer puts together to attract investment, though Carlotti Productions, which produces all my work, is a family concern and our investors are mainly family and friends.' He laughed when she looked none the wiser. 'To answer your question, we're planning a first shoot in May. But the fact that we've finished shooting this present film doesn't mean it's finished. Next the cutting-room and sound studio take it over and start knocking it into shape—while I bite my nails and hurl abuse.'

'I think that's how I'd feel if I were you,' stated Tessa gravely. 'I'd be terrified they'd ruin it.'

He threw back his head and laughed. 'Like my producer, my editor is a cousin of mine who, apart from being one of the best in the business, knows exactly how my mind works…though that still doesn't stop me hurling abuse at him.'

'So you'll be able to have a break before starting your next film,' said Tessa, her eyes drawn to the rich green turbulence of the sea as she wondered whether it could be the idea of returning to London and having to leave all this scenic perfection behind that was making her feel so uncharacteristically depressed.

'Perhaps, but I've a few things to check in connection with the next film while I'm here…and anyway,' he murmured, 'who in his right mind would rush away from all this when he had an excuse to linger on?'

'Who indeed?' sighed Tessa.

'I think I mentioned that the location for this next film is in Donegal.' The wind danced through his hair as he turned and gave her a slow, lazy smile that sent her pulses racing. 'Do you envy me, Tessa?' he teased softly.

Still reeling from the devastating impact of that smile, she pulled a small face when producing an answering smile proved beyond her. 'Need you ask? Of course I do.'

'Good,' he chuckled, 'because that means you'll be all the more likely to agree to staying on a while longer to help me with a few notes and… Damn!' He broke off, raising a hand to attract the attention of one of Paolo's camera operators. 'I need to have a word with him about yesterday's rushes. I'll see you back at the hotel later and we can discuss your staying on—OK?'

Tessa nodded and was conscious of elation pounding

through her as she watched his tall, ski-suited figure stride off.

She began walking slowly up the beach, her thoughts churning. She had no right to be feeling like this, she told herself with angry desperation. She might just as well dig a hole in the sand and bury her head in it, for all the difference it would make to the way she was behaving. How could she equate her belief that Angelica hadn't consciously lied to her with her inability to believe that Sandro was in love with Angelica? It just didn't make sense! It was a nasty fact of life that there were men who had no compunction about being unfaithful to the women they loved—and just because Sandro had been so pleasant to her for the past couple of days, it didn't change the fact that he had made such coldly calculating use of her presence when it had suited him...didn't change the fact that he was all too capable of using women—to the extent of staging an engagement to one simply to suit his selfish ends.

All she had come here for was to get material for an article, she reminded herself grimly, and now she was mixed up in all this! Yet, apart from the few pages of disjointed notes she had jotted down after that session with Angelica, she hadn't so much as glanced at the wretched thing.

The first thing she did when she entered her room was get out the folder, and there was an almost mutinous set to her face as she hugged it to her. This was the reason she had come here and nothing had changed, she told herself determinedly, so she might as well get on with it.

She dropped the folder on the bed with a start when the telephone rang.

'Tessa,' murmured Angelica's voice, 'I was wondering if you felt like joining me for tea in my room—I'm in the middle of packing and would love some company.'

'I'm afraid I've rather a lot to do,' Tessa told her, irritated with herself for the note of guilt colouring her words. 'I must check the wardrobe trailer before the drivers arrive...and one or two other things.'

'Never mind, we can have a drink after dinner, though just a quick one as I have to be up at an ungodly hour,' sighed Angelica. 'You never know with the paparazzi, so I shan't be on the same plane as Alessandro.'

Her expression one of frowning wariness when she had replaced the receiver, Tessa retrieved the trailer keys from her bag and slipped them into her pocket. If Sandro chose not to tell the woman with whom he was supposed to be in love that he wouldn't be leaving on any plane tomorrow, it certainly wasn't her place to do so.

She glanced down at the folder on the bed, then picked it up—she knew of a much brighter place than her room where she could work on it, and do so undisturbed.

Deciding to check the trailer later, she made her way to a conservatory leading off one of the smaller, little-used lounges. It was an airy, plant-studded room with a magnificent view of the coastline—and it was always deserted.

Ten minutes after she had settled into redrafting her notes, she snapped shut the folder with a groan of helpless frustration. The whole exercise was a ludicrous charade! She either grew up and accepted the fact that no editor anywhere would have the slightest interest in her laborious attempts to chronicle Sandro's working methods—or she simply related everything Angelica had told her, in the certain knowledge that several papers would readily snap it up. But it wouldn't be her writing skills they would be snapping up, she reminded herself unnecessarily, and the expression on her face was one of utter repugnance.

'So—this is where you're hiding!'

Tessa gave a start of pure terror, then grabbed the folder and slid it under her chair as Sandro strode past her and flung himself down on the chair opposite.

'It's rather pleasant in here,' he said, glancing around. 'The place is virtually deserted—they're all either packing up trailers or their own bags.'

'Actually, that's what I was about to do,' said Tessa, the panic marginally subsiding in her as she took the keys from her pocket. 'Check the wardrobe trailer.'

'You can't run off on me now,' he protested teasingly. 'I need to know how you feel about staying on for a few days—have you thought it over?'

'I—well…not really,' she stammered, thrown to find that she hadn't given it a single thought.

'Tessa, I'd really be most grateful if you could,' he sighed, his boyishly charming smile so disarming as to render almost inconceivable the idea that she might be being ruthlessly charmed. 'You see, there are several small islands off the Donegal coast,' he continued, 'two of which have been offered to us as potential locations and one of which our location manager feels is just about tailor-made for our needs—though there are a few things he's asked me to check out while I have the opportunity.'

'I thought that was the sort of thing the producer of a film would deal with, not the director,' said Tessa, her fascination with the subject easing aside the last remnants of her panic.

'I shall take great delight in telling my cousin Mario what a lazy producer you consider him,' he chuckled. 'Working with family tends to allow for a lot more give and take than is probably usual—but that's the way I like it. Which reminds me,' he muttered, glancing at his watch, then smiling apologetically. 'I'm expecting a call from Mario shortly. Tell me, Tessa, do I get him to send someone here to me,' he asked, batting his eyelids in teasing supplication as he tilted his head to one side, 'or will you rescue me for a while longer?'

'You couldn't possibly expect him to send you a secretary all the way from Italy,' she gasped, not entirely convinced he wasn't joking.

'He's in England till tomorrow,' he murmured innocently, 'so he'd be sending one from there.'

'You're sure it's nothing more complicated than typing up a few notes?'

'I'm certain,' he grinned. 'And admit it, Tessa, only the other day you made some very unkind remarks to Paolo about my terrible memory.'

Tessa felt her cheeks flame at the soft sound of his laughter.

'You know what they say about eavesdroppers,' she accused, certain that Paolo hadn't repeated her words. 'And anyway, I doubt if there's anything wrong with your memory—your trouble is that you're so used to Carla spoon-feeding you that you've simply got out of the habit of using it.'

'Perhaps a few more days of your tender mercies would cure me,' he murmured, his expression deadpan. 'For heaven's sake, Tessa, I'm teasing you,' he protested in response to the wary look she gave him. 'But I really would be most grateful if you would agree to help me out.'

'Well, the idea of your cousin sending someone over from England seems crazy,' she hedged, and wondered why she was being so ridiculous. There was only one article she could write on him that would get into print— and it was one to which she could never stoop.

'Tess, all I want is a yes or no,' he pleaded, glancing again at his watch. 'I didn't check in with Reception, so if I don't go now I'm likely to miss Mario's call.' He rose to his feet. 'So—what's it to be?'

'I'll stay on.' She was out of her mind—a fact she accepted the instant she heard herself utter those words.

'You're an angel!' he exclaimed, reaching out and running his forefinger lightly down her cheek before moving towards the door. 'I really am sorry I have to dash off like this, but we'll celebrate with champagne at tonight's farewell do—that's a promise!'

'What farewell do?' asked Tessa, swinging round in her chair.

'I was exaggerating—we'll probably all get together after dinner for a few drinks...Paolo will no doubt fill you in on some of the wild end-of-shooting flings we've had in the past,' he chuckled as the Italian appeared beside him in the doorway.

'Later,' grinned Paolo. 'But the driver of the wardrobe trailer, he like to see you, Tessa—he wishes to leave tonight if he can.'

Tessa leapt to her feet. 'I was just off to check the trailer!' she exclaimed, brandishing the keys.

'You come back and have coffee after with me and Sandro in this nice place?' he asked.

'I'll join you once I've spoken to Mario,' Sandro told him, and was repeating himself in Italian when Tessa sped past them.

'I'll try to,' Tessa called over her shoulder. 'Sandro—you're going to miss that phone call!'

It was on her way to breakfast the following morning that the desk clerk waylaid her.

'This found its way here, Miss Morgan.' She smiled as she handed Tessa her folder. 'It seems you left it in the conservatory last night.'

'Oh…thanks, Molly,' said Tessa, her blood running cold—it had gone clean out of her mind!

She returned it to her room and had almost finished breakfast when Sandro entered the dining-room. Dressed in a bulky, crew-necked navy sweater and jeans that had every appearance of having been tailor-made for his long-legged, lean-hipped body, he had an air of a disgruntled sleepwalker about him that reminded her of how quickly she had learned it was something of a joke among his crew that, no matter how hard he tried to mask the fact, he was seldom at his best in the mornings.

'Morning,' he growled unsmilingly, pulling out a chair and flinging himself down on it.

Obviously this was one morning he wasn't about to make any attempt to mask anything, thought Tessa wryly.

'What happened to you and Paolo last night?' she asked. 'I thought we were all supposed to be having a farewell drink.' Not to mention the champagne she had been promised, she added wryly to herself.

'We got tied up with other things,' he muttered, then

glanced vaguely in the direction of the coffee-pot. 'I take my coffee black and with two sugars.'

'Really?' murmured Tessa, irritation flaring in her, partly because of the utter boorishness of his behaviour but also because her pulses had gone on racing despite it. 'I take mine white and without sugar.'

Flashing her a murderous look, he reached out for the coffee-pot and swore under his breath when he discovered it was empty.

Just as he was turning, no doubt to roar for service, Tess concluded uncharitably, a waiter appeared at his side with a fresh pot and a cheery greeting.

'I hate to think how poor Paolo must be feeling,' remarked Tessa, deciding she had to do something to break the stifling silence as he poured his second cup of coffee several minutes later.

'Why?' muttered Sandro, his attention solely on the sugar he was ladling into his cup. 'Did something happen to him?'

'No!' she exclaimed exasperatedly, regretting not having left the silence intact. 'It's just that I assumed the pair of you must have had quite a late night of it...and Paolo had to be up so early.'

'Which only goes to show what a pig I can be to work for,' he drawled, mocking challenge in the eyes meeting hers over the rim of his cup. 'Are you worried I'll keep you up past your bedtime, Tessa?'

'Sandro, if there's any particular reason for your behaving like a...like this,' she said, biting back an insult as she strove to hang on to her temper, 'I'd be grateful if you'd come out with it.'

'What, bare my soul to you, Tessa darling?' he drawled. 'Now, wouldn't that be fun?'

'Am I to take it that the only reason you've been behaving civilly to me for the past couple of days is because you needed a secretary?' she asked quietly.

She was startled by the anger that flashed to his face and more than a little disturbed by the ease with which he managed to erase it.

'My, you really do have a low opinion of me,' he murmured. 'But if you want to chicken out of our agreement, why not simply come out and say so?'

'I happen to be one of those people who, if they say they'll do something, does it,' she retorted haughtily, while inwardly reeling from the change in him. 'And if I want to say something, I tend to say it unless it's unprintable.'

'I'd say that most things were considered printable these days, wouldn't you agree, Tessa?' he enquired with steel-edged mildness as he glanced down at his watch, then, giving her no chance to respond, added, 'I think it's time we thought about getting a move on—we've quite a few kilometres to cover.'

Tessa gave him a startled look. 'I thought you said this island was off the Donegal coast!' she exclaimed, but that wasn't exactly what was on her mind. She had formed a picture of herself remaining at the hotel, perhaps dealing with the odd telephone call or two in his makeshift office, while Sandro went off and did whatever it was he had to, returning now and then to dictate the notes that she would duly type out for him... obviously he had a different picture in mind.

'It is,' he replied, 'but the island, apart from being much further west, is by no means the only location we'll be using. I've decided to check them all while I'm here.' He picked up his cup and drained it. 'As we'll be going well off the beaten track, Molly on Reception has promised to dig out a decent map of the county—I hope you're good at navigating.'

'Navigating?' exclaimed Tessa. 'I've never tried it.' And she had already witnessed enough of the explosive shortness of his temper to realise her fate should she make a hash of it. 'Perhaps it would be better if I drove and you navigated,' she suggested tentatively.

'And perhaps it wouldn't,' he retorted. 'We'd probably never find our way out of Rathmullan.'

'My God, I don't believe this!' exploded Tessa. 'Unspeakably inferior though we women obviously appear to you, there are a few of us who are actually capable of driving a car with a degree of competence!'

'How well or otherwise you drive is immaterial,' he informed her blandly. 'It's my inability to read a map that has to be taken into consideration.'

'Don't be so silly—of course you can read a map,' snapped Tessa. 'Why can't you simply admit—?'

'OK, I admit it—I don't believe women possess the brains to drive a car—happy?' he drawled. 'But that doesn't alter the fact that I have a slight problem known as dyslexia—which, I suspect, would render my attempts at map-reading laborious, to put it somewhat mildly.'

'I...you what?' stammered Tessa, her earlier words of scorn ringing accusingly in her ears.

'I dare say if a dire emergency arose, and our lives depended on my reading a map,' he murmured reassuringly, 'I'd manage to work out some way of doing so—but as things stand I think you'll agree we'd be better off with you doing any navigating we may require.'

'Of course,' gulped Tessa and, in an effort to quash

once and for all those last dregs of suspicion lingering tenaciously in her, began apologising profusely. 'Sandro, I really am sorry. I—' She broke off with a gasp as a thought suddenly occurred to her. 'You read my notes on the markers!' she burst out accusingly.

'For heaven's sake, I said I had a slight problem with dyslexia, not that I was a complete illiterate,' he snapped. 'And, for your information, I didn't read your notes, I merely glanced through them…and anyway, they were full of diagrams.'

'But you could have read the notes had you wanted to—couldn't you?'

'Would it matter if I couldn't?'

'No—of course not!' protested Tessa, floundering with embarrassment while he looked on with an amused detachment that made her suspect he might be enjoying a private joke at her expense.

'Well, to set your mind at rest, yes, I could have read them back. It's my own notes I have problems with—which is why you'll be doing it for me.'

'You mean you can read but not write?' puzzled Tessa.

He rose to his feet, his face contorted with amusement. 'Tessa, not only can I read, but I can also write—happy? But the fact is that too often when I'm forced to take my own notes I find them impossible to decipher—which is why I play safe and rely on Carla, or in this instance you, to take them for me.' He glanced once again at his watch, his expression impatient. 'We really ought to be making a move soon—will fifteen minutes be long enough for you to get your things together?'

'My things?'

'You'll need an overnight bag—in fact, you'd better

bring enough to tide you over for a couple of nights, just in case.'

'Sorry, but I…I don't quite understand,' she stammered. And little wonder, she rounded on herself furiously, considering how she had waltzed into this without so much as a single query as to what it might entail. 'I thought we'd be staying here…at this hotel, I mean.'

'We'll use this place as a base,' he replied, his eyes narrowing to a cold, disconcerting watchfulness as he spoke. 'There's no point in our ferrying ourselves back and forth across the county if we can get into a place near the island.'

'No…I suppose there isn't,' muttered Tessa, with no discernible conviction, as she rose to her feet. 'I'd better get my things together.'

He reached out and placed his hand on her arm as she made to move past him.

'I can't tell you how glad I am to find you're not the sort of person to chicken out once she's made an agreement…I really can't.'

Tessa shook free her arm and walked from the room without a word. The element of threat she felt she had detected in those apparently innocuous words could, perhaps, have been simply her imagination…but not the cold malevolence she had glimpsed in his eyes.

CHAPTER FIVE

ON THE morning of the third day, Tessa was clutching a cup of coffee to her lips and doing her utmost to blend in with the upholstery of the sofa on which she was huddled as Sandro strode towards her across the funereally dark lounge of the small hotel somewhere in the wilds of north-west Donegal.

'So this is where you are.' There was a note of accusation in his surly greeting. 'I thought you must still be in bed. Aren't you having breakfast?'

'This is my breakfast,' retorted Tessa, taking another gulp from the cup. She might have guessed that on the one morning she felt like death he would contrive to breeze in looking almost human for a change, she thought irritably. 'And which particular bed did you think I'd still be in?' she enquired caustically as resentment flared in her.

'Ah—the beds,' he muttered, then flung himself down on a chair. 'Sorry about that.'

'Sorry?' hissed Tessa, having failed to detect the slightest trace of sorrow in either his tone or the unconcerned smile he had flashed her. 'You're *sorry*? Not content with hauling me up and down mountains till I'm giddy with exhaustion, you keep me up half the night reading back two days' worth of notes just to make sure I haven't missed anything and then—'

'Oh, so it's overwork that's put you in this disgusting

mood,' he said. 'I thought perhaps it was last night you were upset about.'

'You're wrong, Sandro, I'm not upset about last night—I'm practically gibbering with rage over it. And it wasn't so much last night as the early hours of this morning!'

'Tessa, must you shout?' he protested, wincing. 'You know I'm not up to this sort of thing at this early hour.'

'Oh, I *am* sorry,' raged Tessa. 'How exactly do you think I feel? When I do eventually fall into bed, in what can only be described as a state of exhausted stupor, I find you pounding on my door minutes later—complaining that your damned bed's too soft!'

'I've already explained,' he protested irritably. 'I wouldn't have involved you had I not been unable to get it through to the man on Reception that I wanted to change my room...he didn't seem to understand English.'

'He probably understood only too well,' exploded Tessa, 'but decided, and rightly, that only a raving lunatic would start demanding to have his hotel room changed at two o'clock in the morning, simply because the mattress didn't suit him! What do you think this place is—the Ritz?'

'So how did you persuade him to give you another room?' enquired Sandro, his tone, and the way in which his glance kept straying towards the rain-bleared windows, indicating only minimal interest in the subject.

'I didn't,' replied Tessa from between clenched teeth, incensed by his demeanour. 'One way or another you probably frightened the wits out of the poor old man, for he was nowhere to be seen when I went looking for him.'

'So where did you sleep?' he asked, his boredom momentarily abating.

'Where do you think I slept?' demanded Tessa. 'I had no option but to use your bed—seeing that you were fast asleep in mine by the time I got back to my room!'

'I wondered who it was who'd flung all my things into—or, to be exact, across—the room.'

'Just consider yourself lucky I'm such a poor aim,' retorted Tessa, returning her cup to the tray beside her before she succumbed to an almost irresistible urge to hurl its contents at him.

'God, no wonder you're in such a foul mood,' he murmured with blatant insincerity, rising, 'after a night in that wretched bed. You should have climbed in beside me,' he added with a theatrically lascivious look. 'You'd have been more than welcome.'

Tessa felt as though a panic button had been hit somewhere inside her. So far she had succeeded in ruthlessly blanking her mind and taking each day as it came…but only because he had made it possible, she thought wretchedly, by neither giving her looks nor making any remarks such as those he had just now.

'I…there was nothing whatsoever wrong with that mattress,' she stammered, all memory of the ghastly, smothering softness on which she had had so little sleep deserting her as she felt the colour blaze mortifyingly to her cheeks.

'You're blushing, Tessa,' he observed smugly, stepping over her feet and seating himself beside her.

'If I am it's with anger,' she retorted defensively, tension racking her as he causally placed an arm across her shoulders. 'And I'll be even more angry if you don't remove your arm from me and yourself from this sofa,' she added in tones which she felt sickening certain betrayed the sudden excitement jangling riotously through her.

'Am I not to be given a chance to apologise?' he protested softly, tilting his head sideways till it rested against hers. 'And to tell you what adventures I've arranged for us today?'

'Whatever it is, it's probably something I'll refuse point-blank to do,' she quavered, her vocal cords refusing to co-operate.

'What makes you say that?' he chuckled, his words a soft breath on her hair as his fingers began toying idly against the curve of her shoulder.

'The lengths you seem prepared to go to charm me into agreeing to whatever it is you're scheming—that's what!' she retorted hotly, remembering the times, during the past couple of days, when he had resorted to the blatant use of charm to manipulate her into doing what he wanted. But at least it had been a charm free of any hint of sexuality, she remembered with a sharp pang of nostalgia. 'You were all sweetness and light when you talked me into being dragged up the side of that mountain—'

'Tess, my sweet, it was a midget of a hill.'

'And you were nauseatingly pally just before—'

'Pally?' he echoed with an incredulous laugh. 'That's something I've never been accused of being,' he added as though grossly insulted.

'Well, I've just accused you of it!' retorted Tessa distractedly, while the beat of the fingers drumming against her shoulder throbbed through her entire body.

'But "pally" most certainly doesn't describe how I feel at this very moment,' he protested with a soft chuckle, his free hand grasping her chin and forcing her to face him. 'Nor you—unless I'm grossly mistaken.'

'Well, you are—mistaken, that is!' The words came out in a distracted squeak.

'But you do understand how I'm feeling,' he teased, tilting up her face. 'You must do if you're able to tell me I'm mistaken in thinking you're similarly afflicted.'

In the instant before his mouth took possession of hers, she was already bracing herself, her nails digging painfully into the palms of her hands to prevent her arms rising to cling around him. She heard the soft growl of laughter in his throat as his lips tried unsuccessfully to coax hers open, and felt the sting of her nails gouging deeper into her flesh as control began slipping from her.

'Come on, Tessa,' he coaxed, his mouth drawing back from her tightly clamped lips. 'We both know you're no ice maiden, so why go to all this bother pretending you are?'

'Irresistible though you obviously believe yourself to be,' she ground out, her eyes almost crossing as she kept them trained on the tanned smoothness of his left cheek, 'I'm afraid I don't find you so.'

'Tessa, are you actually trying to tell me you don't lust after my manly body?' he exclaimed in a parody of incredulity, drawing even further back from her.

'That's precisely what I'm telling you,' she lied, an uneasy blend of relief and disappointment flooding her that he hadn't simply renewed the onslaught she knew she couldn't have resisted for much longer.

'Are you quite sure about that?' he asked, his hands sliding slowly down from her shoulders, halting only when they reached and then casually cupped her breasts.

'I...just what do you think you're doing?' she

squeaked, aghast, as every nerve in her body leapt to riotous life beneath those lean, tanned and elegantly long-fingered hands.

'I'm simply demonstrating how easy it is to prove you a liar,' he murmured with a lightness contrasting markedly with the dark warmth stirring in the depths of his eyes, 'and, of course, reassuring myself that I haven't lost my touch.'

And just in case she might have had any doubts as to the point he was making, his hands began moving in open caress against the peaked rigidity of her blatantly responsive breasts.

It was only when a frantic inner voice silently called out to her that her stunned lack of reaction might easily be mistaken for acquiescence that, with an almost animal howl of outrage, she found the strength to twist her body free from the inciting ministrations of those hands.

'What's your problem, Tessa?' he drawled, the chill in his words reflected in the darkly hooded eyes now gazing disdainfully down into hers.

'My problem?' she croaked, anger eroding her stunned confusion. 'With an ego that seems to demand that any female within striking distance must succumb to your charms, you're the one with the problem, I'd say!'

'Perhaps, after you've weaned me from Carla's alleged spoon-feeding, that's another of my shortcomings you can sort out for me,' he murmured with a brittle smile. 'Though I really must point out that, far from squandering my limitless charms on any woman within striking range, I happen to be exceedingly fussy over such matters.'

Tessa felt a wave of hopelessness sweep over her. She

had no right to be here, she thought numbly. She had succumbed to an almost fatalistic attraction in coming here and with total disregard for any possible consequences.

'One of the many differences between us, Tessa,' he stated in reproving tones, 'is that, whereas I'm able to work out a fair amount of what's going on in your head, I doubt if you ever have the slightest idea what's going on in mine.'

Tempted to retort that it was her own head that she hadn't the slightest idea what was going on in, Tessa leapt to her feet and walked over to the small window.

'Would it be too much to hope that you'll eventually get round to telling me what you have lined up for us today?' she demanded, trying desperately to calm herself as she peered with difficulty through the rain-washed glass, and decided that if it involved traipsing round the countryside he could count her out—only a madman would choose to go out in weather like this.

'I'm sure you'll be glad to hear that I've seen all I need to of the mainland,' he said, joining her at the window. 'It's a shame the weather's so bad that we can't even see the island—they say it's only about eight or nine miles off the coast,' he muttered, then turned, leaning back against the sill and grinning down at her. 'Never mind; we'll be able to see our fill of it once we're there. And the good news is that, instead of us having to be ferried back and forth, there's a guest house we can stay in—I contacted them earlier and made the necessary arrangements.'

Tessa's heart lifted momentarily with the prospect of having the rest of the day to catch up on sleep, then plummeted as a suspicion crept into her mind.

'Sandro, what exactly will we be doing today?' she asked, no hint of that dreadful suspicion entering her tone.

'I've just told you!' he exclaimed impatiently. 'We're going over to the island. In fact, it's about time we got our things together,' he added, glancing down at his watch, 'as the guy who's running us over wants to leave in about half an hour.'

'You're joking!' gasped Tessa, her untenable suspicions confirmed. 'Tell me you're joking!'

'Why the hell should I be joking?' he retorted, plainly irritated.

'Because there's a force heaven knows what gale blowing out there, that's why!' cried Tessa, leaning forward and pressing her face against the glass. 'And even if it weren't for this rain teeming down, I doubt if the island would be visible anyway, thanks to the height of the waves leaping around out there.'

'Don't be so silly,' he snapped. 'The person we're getting a lift with was going over anyway—which he'd hardly be doing if it involved risk.'

Tessa moved away from the window, the idea of actually being on that churning grey turbulence making her feel slightly queasy.

'If ferrying people across to the island is the poor man's livelihood,' she protested, 'he probably can't afford to refuse to take us.'

'Tessa, if you have some sort of hang-up about boats, you should have said so earlier,' he muttered, striding angrily past her towards the door.

'I have no hang-ups whatever,' she informed him icily, not even bothering to attempt to work out why such an outlandish idea had even occurred to him, 'in connection with boats or anything else.'

'If that's so, I suggest you start cultivating one over your complete lack of logic,' he drawled, turning in the doorway. 'The guy who's giving us a lift over happens to be the local veterinary surgeon, but even if he had been a ferryman, it's utterly illogical to suggest that a man whose livelihood depended on a boat would risk taking it out in dangerous weather conditions.'

'How fortunate I am to have a paragon of logic such as yourself around to point out my dreadful shortcomings in that department,' snapped Tessa and, deciding she had had enough, marched straight past him and out of the room.

'Where are you going?' he called after her.

'To get my things together,' she called back, gratified to have heard what she felt had been alarm in his tone. 'It wouldn't do for us to miss the boat, now would it?'

'Did you teach here on the island before you retired, Mrs Maguire?' asked Sandro, apparently thoroughly at ease as he bestowed yet another of his dazzling smiles on their hostess, while the three of them took tea before a magnificent fire in Mrs Maguire's elegant little drawing-room.

'Dear me, no, Mr Lambert,' murmured the elderly lady, her frosty exterior having long since melted beneath the relentless barrage of charm to which it had been subjected. 'It's many a year since this island had a school of its own. In fact, nowadays this is more a place where we islanders who have roamed afar come to spend our retirement years in tranquillity.'

Tessa sat huddled beside the fire in virtual silence as

her two companions exchanged pleasantries, her frozen body avidly replenishing its lost heat while her mind did its best not to dwell on the nightmare sea crossing that had brought her here.

Making a concerted effort to look as though she was capable of contributing to the conversation if called upon, Tessa took discreet stock of their, for want of a better word, hostess. Winifred Maguire was a somewhat forbidding and plainly highly educated woman of around seventy—and just about the last person Tessa would have expected to be running a guest house on this remote island. And Mrs Maguire had not been in the least happy to discover that her guests were of differing sexes, mused Tessa, remembering the old lady's sharp remark about having expected two men.

'You look as though you've had the stuffing knocked out of you,' Mrs Maguire remarked to her with a faint trace of sympathy. 'That trip to the mainland can be a devil in good weather, but with gales brewing as they are now—rather you than me,' she added with a chuckle. 'More tea?'

'No, thank you,' smiled Tessa, feeling physically and mentally drained and unable to keep her mind from thoughts of falling into a bed and the bliss of sleep.

'You need to recover your land legs, my dear,' chuckled the old lady, 'and the only way to do that is to relax and let them return of their own accord.' She turned to Sandro. 'And there's no way she can do that until she's settled in and able to put her feet up. Sean Sweeny's already left your bags over at the cottage—I'll get him to take you both round there.' She rose to her feet, completely missing the look of utter bemusement on Tessa's face. 'Sean and his wife, Maggie, keep an eye on the place while James Merrick, the owner, is away,' continued Mrs Maguire, oblivious of the effect her words were having on Tessa. 'Maggie does the cleaning and will come round and cook your evening meal—she's a good, plain cook.'

Feeling like a mechanical toy whose batteries were fast running down, and with the thought lurking somewhere in the depths of her mind that this was all just a bad dream, Tessa got back into her spray-sodden anorak. Seconds later she found herself once again on the harbour road, doubled up against a wind that seemed to have trebled in ferocity during the half-hour she had been out of it.

The walk to the small, stone-clad cottage to which the voluble Sean Sweeny led them was a good quarter of a mile, and Tessa's feelings of being caught up in a dream were enhanced when her companions struck a common chord and fell into animated conversation. Sean had apparently never heard of Sandro's films, a fact which, to Tessa's secret amusement, he declared with a refreshingly candid lack of embarrassment. But they quickly discovered they shared a passion for the old black and white films. A passion they shared with her stepfather, thought Tessa with an acute attack of homesickness as she trudged along beside them.

The cottage was tiny, originally a two up and two down in which a bathroom had been constructed between the two bedrooms and one of the downstairs rooms converted into a kitchen-cum-dining-room. But the only thing that made any significant impression on Tessa was the fire glowing in the sitting-room, reaching out and permeating the entire house with its cheery warmth.

'I do hope you'll excuse me,' she apologised, when Sean started discussing the times his wife would come round, 'but I'm not feeling too well and I'd like to have a rest.'

Without awaiting a reaction from either man, she collected her holdall from the tiny hall and ascended the narrow staircase. By the time she had entered one of the bedrooms, her legs were threatening to give way beneath her and tears of frustration were glittering in her eyes.

There was no way she could be accused of overreacting, she told herself as she stripped off her sodden clothes and replaced them with a warm jogging-suit. She flung herself disconsolately on the bed and tried to collect her thoughts. He had no right to do this to her! All right, so she shouldn't have been here in the first place—but it was pointless agonising over that now. And yes, she was cold and exhausted and her mind had all but seized up on her… But none of those things mattered in the slightest. What mattered was that every instinct she possessed was shrieking out warnings that Sandro was up to something—and whatever it was it certainly wasn't any good.

'How unwell, exactly, are you?'

With a squeak of fright, Tessa rolled over and sat up. She hadn't even heard the door open, yet there was Sandro at the foot of the bed, gazing down at her with a look devoid of anything even remotely resembling concern.

'Didn't anyone ever tell you how rude it is to barge into someone else's bedroom without so much as a knock on the door?' she fumed.

'I'd have thought you'd have realised by now that I'm

far too uncouth for such niceties,' he drawled, his eyes flickering coolly over her tense figure.

Torn between a desire to scream at him to get out and the need to find out what it was he was up to, Tessa scowled up at him in silence.

'I must say, you don't look particularly ill to me,' he observed dispassionately, strolling round to the side of the bed, 'though I suppose looks can be deceptive.'

'Just what are you up to, Sandro?' she hissed, hugging her arms tightly round her drawn-up knees.

'Up to?'

'You know perfectly well what I mean,' she accused. 'You told me we'd be staying in a guest house!'

'And so we are.'

'No, we're not! This is a rented cottage!'

'If you want to split hairs—'

'And what's more you led Mrs Maguire to believe I was a man!'

'My dear Tessa,' he drawled, 'I doubt if even some-one of Mrs Maguire's advanced years could be led into believing you were a man.'

'You're twisting what I said! What do you think you're doing?' she shrieked as he sat himself down on the edge of the bed. 'Get off! Get out of here!'

'Tessa, there's no need to get hysterical—'

'Hysterical? How dare you? You behave like a foul-tempered boor, then you barge your way into—'

'OK, I admit it, I haven't exactly been easy to get on with...I've had things on my mind. But I've work to do here and our being at one another's throats isn't going to help get it done.'

'I'm quite happy to do the work; it's all the lies you've told about coming here—'

'Lies?' he protested. 'Tessa, were you born suspicious or did something happen to make you so?'

Tessa buried her head against her knees. 'There you go again, twisting everything!'

'Damn it, I'm not twisting anything!' he groaned exasperatedly. 'I asked you a perfectly valid question. Take me, for instance—I wouldn't say I was suspicious by nature, but with my background I've had to learn that you can't always take people at face value. Of late I've been finding it increasingly difficult to trust anyone but my closest friends—but with good reason. I merely asked whether you were as suspicious as you appear to be by nature, or if something made you that way.'

Raising her head from her knees, Tessa flashed him a wary look. He was beginning to sound almost human and for some inexplicable reason it was making her aware of how she had been deluding herself. She wasn't suspicious of his motives in bringing her here—she was afraid, in fact terrified that she was about to fall in love with him, and with no chance of his ever reciprocating such a feeling!

'Something made me that way,' she muttered in a daze.

'Are you going to tell me what?'

She shook her head. She could cope with his vile moods, but this sudden switch left her desperately vulnerable.

'Tessa, I had no choice with the accommodation—' He broke off with a muttered oath. 'Hell, you're not afraid I'd force my attentions on you? Tessa, I—'

'Of course I'm not!' she burst out in horror.

'Thank God for that,' he murmured with a chuckle.

It was the relaxed ease behind that laughter, in marked

contrast to her own nerve-jangling tension, that filled her with sudden resentment.

'The only problem I have with the accommodation,' she informed him stiffly, 'is that, given your foul moods, the chances are I'll end up on a manslaughter charge!'

He was laughing as he rose to his feet. 'I'm sure it won't come to that, not now that I've turned over a new leaf.' There was a teasing challenge in his eyes as he gazed down at her. 'And to prove what a reformed character I am, I'll make us some coffee. You unpack and when you come down I'll serve it in front of that magnificent fire.'

'I hate to spoil such a delightful picture,' said Tessa, having tried in vain to rid herself of the soft warmth permeating her as she too rose, 'but I doubt if this place runs to the sort of coffee you like.'

'Very few places do—that's why I carry my own supply,' he grinned.

'You what?' exclaimed Tessa, then startled herself by bursting out laughing.

'I'm almost as fussy about my coffee as I am my women,' he murmured, taking her lightly by the hands. 'Which reminds me—my turning over a new leaf hasn't in any way altered how desirable I find you...especially when you laugh.'

'Sandro,' she protested, his name catching barely coherently in her throat as he drew her slowly to him.

'Do you know how beautiful you are when you laugh, Tessa?' he whispered, lowering his head to hers.

Unable to speak, Tessa instead took a deep, shuddering breath in an attempt to calm herself, only to find the spicy, masculine scent of him affecting her senses like a heady drug.

'Laughter gives you a very special beauty,' he whispered, his arms tightening around her.

'Sandro, I...' Her words were silenced by the beguiling touch of his mouth on hers. But it was a touch that swiftly ignited to passion as her own lips parted in unconscious welcome. And the fear that stabbed through her with the sudden, almost fatalistic acceptance of how close she already was to loving him was instantly smothered beneath the surge of need pounding inexorably through her.

'I want you, Tessa...I need you,' he groaned indistinctly against her trembling mouth, while his hands slid beneath her top to cup the taut fullness of her breasts.

Reason tried to tell her that this savage, aching need possessing them both offered no answer to all those questions left unasked, but reason was no weapon against the war being waged on it by her own body, now responding with a reckless abandon to the growing hunger of his kisses, nor the blatant message of desire in the taut, lean body to which it so wantonly clung.

But the more powerful the need in her grew, the more those unasked questions began taking positive form. Angelica... Her every instinct had always rejected the idea of his loving Angelica, but it was that unanswered question and the sudden urgency in the body steering hers down on to the bed that at last penetrated the madness threatening to overwhelm her.

'No!' she choked, falling back on the bed as she pushed him from her.

'Why?' he protested hoarsely, releasing her instantly and stepping back from the bed.

'Because, I...you were right about something making me suspicious of men,' she protested disjointedly.

'I…it's not them…it's me…I'm always attracted to completely the wrong sort of man!'

'Do you honestly expect me to take a claim as ludicrous as that seriously?' he snapped, his eyes glacial.

'I can't help it if you don't like the truth,' she retorted defensively.

'The truth is precisely what I would like to hear,' he retorted, 'though it's plainly not what you're prepared to give me. Perhaps it was wrong of me to assume that you would follow me in putting your suspicions aside.'

'Your suspicions?' she gasped. 'What possible reason could you have to be suspicious of me?'

But her indignant gaze faltered, then dropped beneath the cool scrutiny of his as the memory of the duplicity she had once contemplated flashed guiltily through her mind.

'Isn't that what can be so unpleasant about suspicion—it's all too frequent irrationality?'

Perhaps, she agreed in miserable silence as she acknowledged the complete irrationality of that momentary stab of guilt…but she could find nothing in the least irrational about her unshakeable suspicion that loving him would bring her nothing but heartbreak.

'Is it irrational of me to suspect that you are in love with Angelica?' she heard herself ask in a tight, strained voice, and recognised instantly the inherent dishonesty with which she had phrased the question.

'Ah—Angelica,' he murmured, ramming his hands into his pockets and gazing down at his feet.

Unaware that she was doing so, Tessa held her breath as she waited for him to continue.

He turned and walked slowly towards the door while

Tessa watched him, her heart plummeting like a lead weight long before he ever reached it.

There had been no earthly reason for her to doubt Angelica's word, but she had—abandoning any pretence of logic as she blindly followed what she claimed were her instincts.

'I'm not ready to talk to you about Angelica...except to say that I'm not in love with her.'

'I...I'm not even sure why I asked,' she lied in a vain attempt to counter the inordinate relief staggering drunkenly through her.

'Aren't you, Tessa?' he asked softly. 'Perhaps we came too close to making love for you not to have asked.' His back had been towards her; now he turned and gave her a wry, almost but not quite mocking smile as he added, 'I think it's time I saw to that coffee I promised us—don't you?'

CHAPTER SIX

TESSA felt only gratitude for the painstaking thoroughness with which Sandro conducted his inspection of every imaginable location on the tiny island that undulated with breathtaking beauty from craggy cliffs to low-lying fields that sprawled to the sands and almost out to sea. Work had become the safety-net that cradled her mind in its welcome demand...except for lulls such as this, she reminded herself uneasily, her slim body bracing once more against the force of the wind ripping across the cliff-top.

She rammed her hands deeper into the pockets of the brightly hued, oversized ski jacket that Sandro had handed her after her drenching on the second day, her eyes straining to compensate for the distortions of the rain as they followed the tall figure pacing the cliff-edge a few metres ahead.

'Sorry, Tessa, but is there any chance of you taking a few more notes?' he called over to her.

'Hang on a moment,' she called back, unzipping the jacket and unearthing her notepad and a pencil from one of its inner pockets.

Shielding the notepad inside the jacket against the rain, she managed, with considerable difficulty, to jot down his wind-born words.

'I'll be with you in a minute,' he called over when he had finished, then walked to the edge of the cliff and began striding along so close to its rim that Tessa found herself almost grinding her teeth as she bit back a cry of warning for him to take care.

She could think of several occasions, before they had come to the island, when she would happily have shoved him over the edge of any cliff handy, she reflected uneasily as she tucked everything back in its place and re-zipped the jacket. Now she was little more than a neurotic mess, fretting over his safety and terrified it was a sign that she was already in love with him!

She saw him turn and begin striding towards her, and found herself wondering at her own perversity in being unable to cope with his having turned over a new leaf. Probably because the effort it was taking him to stick to his good intentions tended to show now and then, she thought wryly...or perhaps because he hadn't made so much as a single advance towards her since his transformation!

'There are just another couple of points I'd like you to jot down before I forget them,' he announced with an apologetic grin as he drew level with her.

Tessa unzipped the jacket once more and dug in the pockets, flustered both by her unguarded thoughts and the effect his proximity was already having on her.

'Here, let me help,' he offered, opening up his own jacket and stepping right up to her. 'I'll shield you from the wind while you use my chest to lean against.'

Cocooned in the jacket he held around her and having to battle to keep her mind on what she was doing and away from the fact that she was practically in his arms—a thought she was finding inordinately appealing—Tessa took down the words he uttered in that succinct verbal shorthand to which she had so quickly grown accustomed.

'Did you get all that?' he asked finally, the sudden lowering of his head bringing the black wetness of his hair into contact with the golden dampness of hers.

'Yes, but I'm not that sure about what I took down a few minutes ago,' she admitted, then glanced up at him in surprise as he removed the notepad and pencil from her hands and placed them in one of his pockets.

'I'm sure you've enough of the gist of it to jog my memory,' he said. 'We'll check later.'

'Talking about jogging your memory reminds me,' she said as they set off towards the path that snaked its way through the fields and onwards towards the village, 'I owe you an apology. I can't think where I got the idea you had a bad memory—it's fantastic; I'd never have remembered all those details you dictated to me once we got back yesterday.'

'I'm beginning to surprise myself with all I can do without Carla to cosset me.' He laughed, then added anxiously as he gave her a hand over the stone wall leading to the path, 'Not that I have any complaints about your work. I'm most impressed by the way you interpret my ramblings—and then get them on to that computer thing.'

'It's a portable word processor,' corrected Tessa with amusement, 'and so simple a child could use it.'

'Not this child,' he replied, pulling a face. 'Carla reckons I'm not safe around anything even remotely electronic—and I've a feeling she's right.'

Tessa found herself wondering if that could have anything to do with his dyslexia, and felt uncomfortable as she remembered her scepticism when he had first mentioned it. She had still noticed nothing that would support his claim but, warped though his sense of humour could be, she doubted that even he would joke about such a subject.

As they made their way down the path in a companionable silence she wondered why she hadn't simply broached the subject with him…why she found it virtually impossible to broach most subjects, other than those connected with work, with Sandro. But it was as these thoughts were churning worryingly in her mind that the heavens opened up on them and they raced one another to the cottage to collapse drenched and laughing in the hall.

'You can bath first and I'll make the coffee,' gasped Sandro as he began shedding his sodden clothing where he stood.

'Are you sure?'

'To the bath!' he ordered, kicking off his shoes and revealing long, perfectly shaped and darkly tanned legs as he nonchalantly stepped out of his trousers.

'No, *I'll* do the washing-up,' insisted Sandro. 'You laid the table and dished up the meal. My mamma holds very strong views on household democracy,' he informed her with a pious look, which he immediately ruined with a mischievous grin, 'and raised me accordingly.'

Tessa had serious doubts as to the accuracy of such a claim; he was plainly used to being waited on hand and foot. But she felt a warm, tingling feeling pervade her none the less—it was the first reference he had made to the mother he was reputed to adore and she couldn't help regarding it as a promising omen.

'All right,' she agreed, 'but it's only fair that I make the coffee.'

The look of alarm she had anticipated duly flitted

across his handsome features and she found herself having to stifle laughter. Sandro's attitude to coffee, she had quickly discovered, bordered on reverential and the pot she had brewed that morning hadn't, to put it mildly, gone down too well.

'No—I'll make it,' he said, pausing only fractionally as he did a bit of quick thinking. 'You can build up the fire…it would be terrible if it went out.'

'It would—but I can easily cope with both,' she replied innocently. 'Or didn't you like the coffee I made you this morning?'

'I—' He broke off, pulling a threatening face at her when he saw the struggle she was having against laughter.

'No, I didn't,' he growled, 'but I'm far too well brought up to mention it!'

'Of course you are,' chuckled Tessa, 'but the moment you thought my back was turned you ran to the sink, clutching your throat, and spat it out!'

'The fire!' he roared, his laughter following her as she sped from the room.

It was as she put a log and more coal on the fire that her laughter was gradually replaced by a soft, decidedly dreamy smile—a smile that died the instant she became aware of it.

This was what had so terrified her, she thought numbly, sitting back on her heels and gazing sightlessly into the flickering flames. She had spent a day freezing in gale-force winds and had been drenched to the skin…and she had never felt happier in her entire life.

'Tessa, I'm afraid I have a slight problem.'

She started as the sound of his voice from the doorway dragged her from her disquieting thoughts.

'What—you can't manage both the washing-up and the coffee?' she asked, only just managing to inject teasing lightness into her words.

'No, I... that first-aid box fit for a hypochondriac you mentioned coming across the other day—where is it?'

It was something in his tone that brought Tessa leaping to her feet and it was a shriek of combined terror and horror that escaped her when she caught sight of the blood-soaked tea-towel wrapped around his left hand.

'Sandro! Oh, my God, what have you done to yourself?' she cried, racing over to him.

'I'm sure there's no need to panic,' he muttered wanly, leaning back against the wall as though in dire need of its support.

'I shan't panic!' she lied raggedly, then made a supreme effort to pull herself together as she remembered Angelica's words about his squeamishness at the sight of blood. 'In fact, I'm not in the least likely to panic,' she stated, her voice suddenly imbued with authoritative calm. 'I once started training to be a nurse.'

'What made you stop?' he demanded, his tone almost aggressive.

'A bit of bad luck,' she muttered absently, horrified by his pallor. 'Sandro, come and sit down and let me have a look at it,' she urged, praying he wasn't about to pass out on her as she took him by the arm and led him to the sofa. 'Tell me what happened,' she continued unhurriedly while she attempted, without success, to draw down the hand he was holding protectively to his chest.

'I'm not too sure,' he muttered vaguely. 'There must have been a particularly sharp knife in among the things in the washing-up bowl.'

'I'll go and get that first-aid box,' she stated, unsaying

her prayers that he wouldn't pass out—if he did, at least she would have a chance to inspect the damage before he bled to death!

All he had done was cut his hand, she kept chanting to herself as she went to the kitchen and got out the first-aid box. She placed it on a tray together with a bowl of the water he had boiled for the coffee. She paused as she went to lift the tray, gazing down at her badly shaking hands and remembering how, in her days as a student nurse, her ability to distance herself and remain calm had been such a godsend. Now, not only was she incapable of distancing herself from what Sandro might be suffering, she was suffering it tenfold herself!

He was still seated as she had left him when she returned and placed the tray on a small table which she drew up beside the sofa. And he remained gazing morosely into the fire when she sat down beside him, his hand still clutched to his chest.

'Let me have a look,' she said gently, no part of her stopping to question the love surging like a tidal wave within her.

'It's OK—I'll see to it myself in a few minutes,' he growled uncooperatively.

'No, you won't,' she insisted firmly. 'I'll see to it now.'

'Tessa, if you really must know, I don't want you around…simply because I'm the biggest wimp there is when it comes to the sight of blood.'

'Obviously it's just as well I am here,' she replied, fighting an almost overwhelming urge to put her arms round him and comfort him as she reached over and drew his now unresisting hand down on to her knee.

'And it's perfectly natural to be disturbed by the sight of blood.'

'Not the way I'm disturbed, it isn't,' he muttered, making a half-hearted attempt to withdraw his hand as she made to unwrap it. 'What are you doing?' he demanded suspiciously.

'I'm just going to have a look at it,' she replied, 'but perhaps it's best if you don't.'

'I shan't faint, if that's what you're worried about,' he muttered. 'I'd be more likely to deposit my supper all over us.'

'If that's the case, it really would be better if you didn't look,' murmured Tessa, finally succeeding in unwrapping his hand and having to make a conscious effort not to flinch as she exposed what appeared to be a very deep gash across the base of his thumb. 'Heaven only knows how you managed to do that!' she exclaimed shakily, then quickly added, 'But I doubt if you'll die from it.' She lightly re-wrapped his hand before turning her attention to the contents of the first-aid box, just in case he was tempted to take a look. 'I'll give the wound a good clean—to make sure it doesn't become infected.'

His reply was a half-hearted grunt, but she was glad that he kept his face turned away as she began her initial cleaning with cotton wool and the boiled water—at least there was no chance of his seeing how badly her hands were shaking.

'That's good,' she murmured, when she started gently disinfecting the wound. 'The bleeding's just about stopped.'

'I'm glad to hear it,' he said in a decidedly strained voice. 'When I was a kid I always associated the sight of blood with imminent death...probably because as a six-year-old I saw a man bleed to death.'

'My God—how dreadful!' exclaimed Tessa.

'It was a traffic accident and the poor devil was flung through the windscreen. Nasty little tyke that I was, I was at first fascinated by the sight of all that blood— then I heard someone say he'd died...' His words petered out.

'Witnessing something that horrible, and when so young, was bound to affect you,' said Tessa, trying not to show any visible reaction as she examined the now clean wound—a doctor, she felt certain, would have recommended a few stitches.

'What—and still be affecting me twenty-five years on?' he asked irritably.

'For heaven's sake, loads of adults have hang-ups over all sorts of things!' Tessa exclaimed, placing a sterile pad over the wound. 'And it's not as though you're useless in an emergency,' she added, taping the pad neatly in place.

'What makes you say that?'

Tessa glanced up from what she was doing and found herself looking into a pair of disconcertingly watchful eyes.

'Angelica happened to tell me how bravely you acted when her brother had his accident,' she replied, wanting to kick herself for having let such a remark slip out.

'I wonder what else Angelica just happened to tell you?' he drawled. 'I do hope she didn't forget to let you know how delightfully I reacted after my superman act.'

'She didn't forget to!' exclaimed Tessa exasperatedly. 'But how could that possibly detract from what you'd done? For heaven's sake, what is it with you men and your wretched image of yourselves? If it's any comfort, I think you've been terribly brave and macho during the past few minutes—not a single tear in sight!'

For an instant he looked at her as though she had lost her mind, then he burst out laughing. 'At least no one could accuse you of pandering to my fragile ego.' He chuckled, lifting his bandaged hand from her lap and looking down at it as though not quite convinced that it was still a part of him. 'But thank you for a most professional job…I think I'll go and make that coffee now.'

'You most certainly will not!' exclaimed Tessa, rising to her feet and collecting up the things she had used. 'What you'll have to drink is a glass of water—laced with a couple of aspirins.'

He was still protesting half-heartedly when she picked up the tray and carried it to the kitchen.

It was the uncontrollable shaking of her hands as she tidied the things away that made it impossible for her mind to maintain the rigid blankness she had tried to impose on it.

All right, so he probably did need a couple of stitches in the cut, but that could be seen to in the morning, she argued frantically with herself. Then her shoulders sagged with defeat as she felt the tears start to stream down her cheeks.

'I don't want to be in love with him,' she protested in a despairing whisper. 'I need it like a hole in the head!'

Unsettled to find that she was talking aloud to herself, she gave an angry scrub at her face, then let out a groan of frustrated incredulity when her hand began tingling with a familiar painfulness.

There was actually a pack of disposable gloves in the

first-aid box, she remonstrated with herself as appalled awareness hit her. And she, who had had to give up nursing because of her wretched allergies, hadn't even thought to use them!

Muttering feverishly to herself, she rummaged through the exceptionally well-stocked box, a huge sigh of relief escaping her as she found what, in her heart of hearts, she hadn't really expected to—a tube of a salve that would arrest her reaction to the antiseptic she had so thoughtlessly used.

Once she had rubbed the cream into her hands, she dropped a couple of aspirins into a glass of water and returned with it to the sitting-room.

'I'm sure your hand's throbbing quite badly, but this should help alleviate it,' she said as she handed him the glass.

He took the drink and downed it in one gulp, his smile, as he returned the glass to her, turning to an expression of alarm. 'Tessa, what's wrong?' he exclaimed, forgetting himself and wincing as he reached out with his damaged hand and drew her down beside him.

'You must be more careful,' she choked, striving desperately not to make a complete fool of herself as the full impact of the fact that she actually was hopelessly in love with him hit her with a sickening force. 'You could start up the bleeding again...and I think you might need a couple of stitches—'

'Tessa, why are you crying?'

'I'm not!' she protested, then gave a howl of frustration as she made to rub away the tears she had so forcefully denied, only just in time remembering the cream she had rubbed into her hands.

'Tessa, darling, what's wrong?' he pleaded, placing his arm round her and hugging her to him.

'I...I can't even rub my eyes...I've never felt so stupid in all my life!'

He muttered something softly to himself in Italian, then took her chin in his hand, tilting her face upwards. 'Tessa, you're not making too much sense.'

'Of course I'm not—I told you, I'm stupid!' she choked. 'Anyone else with my record would at least have had the sense to use gloves...and there's a whole pack of them in the—'

'Tessa, just slow down,' he ordered. 'Now—tell me why you can't rub your eyes.'

'Because I've got anti-allergy cream all over my hands!'

'And why is that?'

'Because I'm allergic to several antiseptics...that's why I had to give up nursing!'

'And tonight you used one to bathe my hand and your allergy started up!' he exclaimed, at last beginning to see sense in her rambling protestations. 'At least our first-aid box came lavishly enough equipped to contain a counteracting cream—which I'm sure no common-or-garden one would have.'

'Yes...but that isn't the point,' wailed Tessa, the idea forming vaguely in her mind that she really should be doing something about pulling herself together. 'I shouldn't have needed it in the first place—the box also contains a pack of disposable surgical gloves!'

'Oh, I'm sure it does,' he agreed, a hint of laughter in his voice. 'And, if we dug deep enough, we'd no doubt find it also contains a do-it-yourself brain surgery kit.'

He took her head in his hands and, using his thumbs, very gently wiped the tears from her face.

'You shouldn't be using that thumb,' protested Tessa raggedly. 'I've told you the bleeding could start again.'

'Tessa, why are you crying?' he whispered, ignoring her advice.

'I...because this evening reminded me of how much I'd wanted to be a nurse,' she lied disjointedly. What was she supposed to do—admit that it was because she was in love with him, she thought disconsolately, and dreaded the inevitable moment when her heart would be broken?

'But there are other things you could do related to nursing—'

'Yes, I know there are,' she protested with guilty distraction. 'I just don't want to talk about it!'

That was what Charles and her mother had tried to point out to her, but she had been too busy wallowing in self-pity to listen.

'I'm sorry, I didn't mean to upset you,' he said quietly, a slightly guarded expression on his face as he released her. 'Tessa, if I were to instruct you in the art of coffee-making, would it be OK for us to have a cup now?'

She shook her head, melting beneath the sweetness of his sudden, teasing smile. 'You drink your coffee far too strong and what you need is a good night's sleep—you're still as pale as a ghost.' She got to her feet. 'There's some cocoa in the kitchen—if you go to bed, I'll bring you up a nice hot mug of it.'

She laughed as he gave a theatrical shudder.

'Whatever you say, Nurse,' he sighed, rising also. 'Tessa?' he added as she began walking to the door.

She stopped and turned, feeling as though neon lights were flashing out the love churning in tumult within her as she watched him walk towards her.

'Thank you for taking such good care of this,' he murmured, gesturing towards his hand.

For an instant she was so certain he was about to take her in his arms that her heart was already pounding in anticipation. Then he reached out with his undamaged hand and stroked it lightly against her cheek.

'Perhaps you're right about an early night and that cocoa,' he stated almost abruptly, then walked past her and out through the door.

She should count herself lucky that he was no longer physically attracted to her, she told herself angrily as she prepared the cocoa. There had been other men to whom she had been strongly attracted, but the relative ease with which she had resisted those attractions had only strengthened her untested conviction that she was incapable of making love with a man she didn't love…and now, contrary to all reason, she was being consumed by the intensity of a love over which she seemed to have no control, and for just about the last man ever likely to return it.

His bedroom door was open, but only the hall light was on. She tiptoed inside and placed the drink on the bedside table and only then realised that he wasn't in the bed. She turned and saw him silhouetted in the doorway.

'I…I thought you were already in bed,' she said, her breath catching awkwardly in her throat.

'I was brushing my teeth.'

'Toothpaste will make the cocoa taste a bit strange,' she whispered as he walked towards her.

'Why are you whispering, Tessa?'

'I don't know…I…how do you feel?'

'Like I've never felt before,' he replied hoarsely, pulling her into his arms.

It was as though a sudden madness had possessed them both as they clung to one another in a desperation of need. Her mouth responded unreservedly to the torrid siege of his, her lips parting eagerly to the probing invasion of his tongue while his hands impatiently negotiated her clothing to explore feverishly against her flesh.

He groaned out her name as he swung her up in his arms, murmuring unintelligible endearments as they tumbled down on the bed, their mouths clinging in a frenzy of hunger while their bodies became a wild entanglement of the clothing he was stripping randomly from them both.

'I've wanted you too much for too long,' he groaned, his hands like hot velvet against her burning flesh as he removed the last of her clothing. 'Tessa, slow me down if I'm too impatient…but please don't ask me to stop.'

'I don't want you to slow down!' she cried out, her arms reaching imploringly towards him as he flung aside the rest of his own clothes. 'I don't want you to stop!'

But she could feel the strain in him as he tempered the rage of his need and saw it in his eyes in the half-light as he gazed down on her naked, trembling body.

'You're more beautiful than I ever dreamed,' he whispered unsteadily, galvanising her into shuddering life as his hands began tracing a tantalising trail over her body. 'So much more beautiful,' he groaned, sliding down and burying his face against the tingling tautness of her breasts.

She tried to speak, but all that escaped her was a soft moan as her arms reached out and held him fiercely to her. The touch of his mouth, even the moist heat of his breath against her flesh was like an electric shock coursing through her body as she tried desperately to contain the need about to explode within her. She gasped out his name, her entire body tensing almost to snapping-point as the relentlessly inciting play of his mouth and tongue on her almost painfully aroused breasts brought another gasping cry of desperation from her and sent a series of violent shudders blasting through her.

'Sandro,' she pleaded raggedly, her fingers now tugging in his hair with the same restless distraction jarring throughout her entire body.

'Am I hurting you?' he whispered, sliding upwards till he was lying on his stomach beside her, his face only just discernible in the half-light as he gazed down at her.

'No!' she protested vehemently, reaching up and twining her arms frantically around his neck. 'Of course you weren't hurting me! You were…' She shook her head, unable to express the rage of need racking her.

'I was what?' he demanded huskily.

She pressed her body closer to the unyielding planes of his, impatiently drawing his head down towards hers. 'Hold me,' she pleaded, the desperation of her need trembling in her voice.

His reply was a soft growl of satisfaction, then he turned on his side, his arms encompassing her as he drew her trembling body against the muscled length of his.

'You're shivering,' he whispered hoarsely.

'I can't help it,' she choked, now so overwhelmed by the need bombarding her that she was incapable of registering the fact that it was her body's unreservedly eager response to its first contact with the awesome power of an unequivocally aroused male body, rather than any sense of fear, that was causing the violent trembling cascading through her.

'I'm glad you can't help it,' he responded with a throaty laugh, and then began inflicting the most exquisite torture on her entire body.

'Sandro!' she cried out, convinced that her mind was deserting her as the need possessing her became a raging hunger.

'Do you want me to stop?' he demanded huskily, then laughed at the vehemence of her incoherent denial before his mouth resumed its nuzzling punishment. 'Don't ever want me to stop,' he groaned, his hands taking outrageously erotic liberties, teasing and tormenting wherever they chose to stray.

It was when her own hands and mouth began their own eager liberty-taking that his mouth returned in impassioned impatience to hers. And then it was his softly groaned protests that began mingling with hers in the ravenous passion of their kisses, while his body, hampered by the unrestrained impatience of hers, finally gained control and held her spread-eagled beneath him. Yet, as her body tensed in fearless spontaneity to receive him, it was the gentle, mind-blowingly intimate exploration of his hands that brought soft cries of wonderment, mixed with agitated impatience, choking from her.

'I'm not afraid!' she protested, not even conscious of the words pouring distractedly from her as she cried them out again and again.

For an instant his body froze above hers, then he was whispering soft, disjointed words to her in his mother tongue while his hands renewed their maddening, intoxicating onslaught on her body, priming it to a point where the explosive ardency of his possession, when it finally came, was a welcomed joy, so utterly devoid of the pain she had subconsciously expected that it brought a gasping laugh of shocked delight bubbling from her.

'So, you *were* afraid,' he chided huskily, a shuddered laugh escaping him as his body tried to calm the uninhibited urgency of hers, stilling the reckless abandon of its eagerness to the slower, more powerfully contained rhythm of his. But it was a rhythm that grew more reckless with the ardency of the response it met, gradually letting go of the last of its restraint until it was an unfettered force that left them suspended in an exquisite agony of promise that she felt could never possibly be fulfilled. Yet it was even as the soft cries began spilling from her—cries of disbelief at the agonies of pleasure to which she was being subjected mixed with cries of protest that she would be left hovering on this maddeningly exquisite brink forever, incapable of taking just that one final step—that the impossible began happening. Perhaps it was the heightened urgency in his voice when he called out her name that triggered it, or perhaps her body's response to the passion surging almost beyond control in his, but it was a force that engulfed them both, its explosive power fusing within them, lifting and carrying them, holding them suspended in a mindlessness of ecstasy before speeding them towards shattering oblivion with the ferocity of its strength. Then gradually it began piecing them together again, dragging them back to earth on the cushion of the random, softly diminishing echoes of its own explosive glory, till at last they lay locked in limp exhaustion in the sanctuary of one another's arms.

Her mind and body floated in a soporific haze, a dream world in whose seductive balm she would happily have remained forever. But when, with a softly groaned sigh, he eased his weight from her and turned on to his back with her still cradled in his arms, she breathed in the heady masculine scent of him and was filled with the poignant ache of a love beyond words.

'Tessa?'

She acknowledged her name silently, stretching out an arm across the muscled curve of his chest, her skin tingling in delighted awareness of the abrasive sensation of hair beneath it.

'When you said you weren't afraid... Oh, hell, how do I go about this?'

'Go about what?' She buried her face into the damp warmth of the curve of his shoulder, wickedly luxuriating in her certainty as to what the question he was having such difficulty asking was.

'I...Tessa, I'm trying to be diplomatic and you're being most uncooperative,' he complained, his arm tightening around her while he scattered gentle, lazy kisses against her temple.

'You, diplomatic?' she teased contentedly.

'You have to make allowances for the fact that English isn't my first language,' he protested indignantly. 'But, if you insist on being so uncharitable...' He then launched into a husky outpouring—every word of it in Italian.

Their shared laughter lingered on in her when she fell asleep in the circle of his arms. But later, when the explosive sweetness of their mutual need had once more possessed them, it wasn't laughter that was dancing in her heart as, cradled in his arms, she once again found sleep, but a joyous awakening of hope.

CHAPTER SEVEN

'I'VE already slopped some of it, I'm afraid.'

Tessa stirred, then sat up in bed with a sleepy groan that swiftly transformed into a disbelieving gasp as the pleasantly aching sensation permeating her entire body flooded her mind with myriad erotic memories.

'The problem is I forgot to leave room for the milk,' continued Sandro, a frown furrowing his brow as he concentrated on the overflowing mug he was carrying towards the bedside table.

Dragging her eyes from that devastatingly handsome unshaven face for fear that her senses might seize up on her completely, Tessa glanced at his bandaged hand and gave a cry of horror at the sight of the brownish stains on it.

'Sandro, your hand—what's happened?'

'I told you,' he grinned, depositing the mug and sitting down on the bed, 'I've slopped tea all over the place.'

'Tea?' she echoed weakly, glancing towards the drink and trying not to react to the curious black bits floating on its surface.

'I know you prefer tea in the morning,' he stated, taking one of her hands in his and pressing his lips to its palm. 'Good morning, sleepyhead, I trust you slept well.'

Unable to speak for the happiness pounding through her, she leaned forward and rested her head against the silken darkness of his, the fingers of her free hand caressing lovingly in his hair. Even more than the soft kisses nuzzling against her palm, it was the fact that he had actually gone to the trouble of making her tea—or attempting to—that was almost like a declaration of love.

'I'd better get that dressing on your hand changed,' she whispered against his hair. 'Then we'll have to see about finding a doctor to have a look at it.'

'Later,' he murmured, pressing one last kiss on her hand before releasing it and consulting his watch. 'I'm afraid I'll have to get round to Mrs Maguire's place— there's a call coming through for me there in about ten minutes.' He drew her from him, smiling, but there was a smouldering hunger in his gaze.

'Oh,' said Tessa dazedly, feeling she was drowning in the message in his eyes.

'Oh, yes.' He chuckled ruefully. 'It's probably my cousin Mario; he could track down a recluse in the Sahara. Mrs Maguire sent Sean round with a message that someone had rung and would ring back later.' He reached up with his unbandaged hand and gently smoothed her tousled hair back from her face. 'I'd better get going—I'm sure Mrs Maguire won't take in the least kindly to being cast in the role of telephonist.'

'She wouldn't—for anyone else but you, that is,' murmured Tessa, then flung herself against him in a surfeit of love.

'Oh, no.' He chuckled in soft protest, lifting her from him and rising. 'Will-power is something I'm running a little low on right now!'

He deposited a frustratingly chaste kiss on her forehead, then walked to the door.

'Sandro, don't forget to ask Mrs Maguire about a doctor,' she called after him. 'I'd feel a lot happier if one could have a look at your hand.'

'Your happiness, my sweet, is my command,' he said, laughing, blowing her a kiss before he closed the door behind him.

During the hours that had ticked by, Tessa's imagination had gradually led her from one unspeakable horror to another, ranging from his having been knocked down by a speeding car—despite her only ever having seen one car on the island, an ancient contraption worthy of a place in a museum—to his having collapsed with a life-threatening bout of septicaemia. And during those hours she had also gradually toppled from the cloud of delusion on which she had been so blissfully floating. If Sandro had loved her, he would have come straight out with it and said so—that was the sort of man he was. And if he had even cared for her, he wouldn't have left her to agonise like this, hour after terrifying hour…he would have got some sort of message to her.

She stirred herself from the benumbed stupor of her curled-up position on the sofa, glancing listlessly towards the tiny, rain-bleared window before adding more coal to the dying fire. Then her entire body froze to a breath-stifling alertness as she heard the front door open and she waited in agonised apprehension for the sound of Sandro's voice. The sound that she did hear, and then only after a timelessness of waiting, was that of the kettle being filled in the kitchen, followed by the clatter of crockery being taken from a cupboard.

She leaned forward, her knuckles gleaming a deathly white against the dark wood of the mantelpiece she reached out and grasped as nausea swept debilitatingly over her. He knew she wouldn't have gone out, she told herself, her head swimming, yet he hadn't called out to her—hadn't made the slightest attempt to check her whereabouts. So what? taunted a bitter voice within her. She should have known what sort of man she was dealing with—after all, he had never made any secret of what it was he wanted from her. Yet last night and this morning... She shook her head with a violence that trembled through her entire body, then hesitated, torn between fury and desperation... What if he had had terrible news from home? And what if pigs could fly? she vacillated angrily. No one had the right to subject another human being to the hours she had suffered!

He was seated at the table when she entered the kitchen, his unshaven face giving him an almost saturnine appearance as he gazed morosely down at the coffee he was pouring.

'My, that must have been some call,' she stated, her tone oddly pitched as she fought an almost ungovernable urge to scream abuse at him. 'It appears to have lasted the best part of six hours.'

'You're right—it was one hell of a call,' he responded sourly, then reached over and picked up some newspapers from the chair beside him and flung them on to the table. 'The English newspapers came in on the mail boat—I thought they might interest you.'

Tessa looked at him as though he had lost his mind—perhaps he had, she thought with a stab of alarm. But it was with feelings of mounting panic that she turned from him and began going through the motions of making tea while wondering about the precarious state of her own mind.

'By the way,' he drawled in cold, impersonal tones,

'Mrs Maguire's neighbour is a retired doctor—he had a look at my hand and put some stitches in it.'

Tessa, who had been in the process of filling the kettle, hesitated. This was unreal, she thought dazedly...it wasn't happening to her. Oh, but it was, she informed herself harshly as something finally snapped in her and she dropped the kettle and spun round to face him with a howl of outrage.

'Just what the hell do you think you're playing at, Sandro?' she demanded, her voice shaking with fury.

'Why don't you read these?' he retorted, picking up one of the papers and hurling it at her. 'And then tell *me* what the hell you think *you're* playing at!'

Beside herself with rage, Tessa picked up the remaining two papers on the table and flung them in his face.

He leapt to his feet with a bellow of fury. 'You'll read them,' he informed her through clenched teeth, striding towards her and catching hold of her, then forcing her down on to a chair, 'even if I have to tie you down to make sure you do!'

'You're out of your mind!' she screamed, fighting like one demented right up until the moment he locked an arm threateningly around her neck.

'Read the bloody things!' he ordered, his brutal hold tightening momentarily as he stooped to retrieve the paper from the floor and place it with the others before her.

'What will do you if I don't—kill me?' she demanded scathingly.

'Probably—now open the bloody things!'

His vicious hold on her eased marginally as reason persuaded her that she had no option but to comply and she reached for the first of the papers.

'I don't even know what I'm supposed to be looking for,' she protested wearily, both reason and his manic behaviour telling her that it had to be something direly specific.

'I don't think you'll have much difficulty recognising what it is when you come across it,' he snarled, then abruptly released her.

She realised, as she listlessly turned a couple of pages, that it was shock that was making her feel so peculiarly drained; but it was a shock that drained her completely that assailed her when she turned the next page and found herself staring down at a picture of her tormentor and, below it, one of Angelica Bellini smiling serenely into the camera.

'Now open the others,' he ordered icily as the paper slipped from her listless fingers. 'And then read what they have to say.'

Fully aware of the futility of arguing, Tessa lined up the three papers and skimmed through the accompanying articles—each filled with arch and irritatingly clichéd speculation as to why Angelica had joined the director on location in Ireland. In all three articles both Umberto Bellini's accident and Sandro's short-lived and recently broken engagement were rehashed in luridly speculative detail.

Tessa leaned back and closed her eyes as she attempted to sort out the hideous jumble of her mind. This positively unbalanced reaction of his to the press coverage seemed only to confirm Angelica's claims...one of which had been that Sandro was in love with her.

'Well?' he enquired with chillingly soft menace.

Tessa straightened, the beginnings of an anger such

as she had never before experienced stirring within the depths of her.

'What am I supposed to say?' she retorted. 'Surely you've learned by now that this sort of thing is the price people like you have to pay for your fame.'

'And what sort of price would you demand for treachery, Tessa?' he asked, the menace in his tone now a harsh rasp.

Tessa felt her fists clench in response to the white-hot fury now searing through her. To think that she had once had qualms about some of those other men she had been attracted to, she thought incredulously; men who now seemed like saints when compared to the rat on whom she had eventually squandered her love! Sandro was nothing more than an unprincipled lecher who liked to have his cake and eat it and who— Her rampaging thoughts jarred to a violent halt.

'Sandro, does Angelica know that I'm here with you?' she asked in tones devoid of any expression.

'If she didn't, she does now,' he retorted, his eyes narrowing with suspicion, 'your name having cropped up on several occasions during our long conversation this morning...though I dare say she'd have learned about it from the Press soon enough anyway.'

Tessa leapt to her feet, fury overspilling from her.

'And *you* have the nerve to ask *me* about the price of treachery?' she raged. 'It amazes me to discover that you actually possess a shred of conscience, but, now that it happens to have stirred itself, don't try palming your pathetic guilt off on me! The fact that I was stupid enough to let myself be conned by a two-timing, conniving womaniser is more than enough for me to have to live with, so forget about trying to browbeat me with your damned problems, whether they be over the publicity you and your wretched girlfriend don't want or the fact that she's found out what you've been up to behind her back!'

'Have you quite finished?' he drawled, though there was a look of startled confusion in his eyes as they bored into hers.

'Almost, apart from reminding you that you've nothing to gloat over concerning your conquest of me. As I've already told you, I'm particularly attracted to creeps—and you, Sandro, are just about the worst possible creep any woman could have the misfortune to fall foul of!'

He grabbed her by the arm, jerking her to a vicious halt as she made to storm past him.

'Your other creeps must have been a pretty dim lot if that's the sort of stunt you're used to pulling.'

'What do you mean—stunt?' she virtually screamed at him, kicking out at him in fury while she struggled to free her arm.

'Spouting forth a load of drivel, then thinking you can make your grand exit before it's sunk in with the poor mug that you haven't uttered a single intelligible sentence—that's what I mean!' he roared back at her, his eyes blazing as he deftly side-stepped the kick aimed at his shins. 'Though that's no more than the sort of behaviour I'd expect from a sordid little bitch who'd take advantage of someone like Angelica and then feed a pack of lies to her cronies in the gutter press!'

'I…what did you say?' croaked Tessa, her mind balking violently at the only interpretation she could possibly make of his words.

'My God, running into Angelica must have seemed

like Christmas and your birthday rolled into one,' he exploded with disgust.

'And then there was the added bonus of you, Sandro,' she hissed in venomous retaliation to the hurt being inflicted on her, then sank down on the nearest chair as her legs began buckling beneath her.

Those newspaper articles, she thought with dazed incredulity; he held *her* responsible for them! She felt her head swim sickeningly as vivid memories of the previous night began assaulting her senses. It had meant everything to her and nothing to him, she told herself in a desperation of rage and hurt... She had never been able to make Angelica out, but it seemed that all this woman, whom he claimed not to love, had to do was make any outrageous accusation she cared to and he would believe her.

She rose to her feet and glared in warning at him. 'Don't you dare lay so much as a finger on me!'

'What makes you think I'd wish to lay even so much as a finger on you?' he demanded viciously.

'I was referring to your bullying tactics of a few moments ago,' retorted Tessa, only her outraged pride keeping her voice reasonably intact. 'I could hardly be referring to anything even remotely sexual—not now that you've had all you wanted from me in that respect.'

'With a mind that can come up with something like that, it's little wonder you're given to feeding garbage to the Press!' exclaimed Sandro in disgust.

'Tell me, Sandro,' exploded Tessa, having difficulty restraining herself from picking something up and hitting him over the head with it, 'if your precious Angelica told you I mugged old ladies as a pastime, would you have any difficulty believing her?'

'What's that supposed to mean?'

'Work it out for yourself,' she retorted wearily. 'I've better things to do.'

'Such as?' he jeered.

'Such as putting the finishing touches to the work I've done for you, so that I'm ready to catch tomorrow's mail boat back to the mainland.'

'What makes you think there will be a mail boat in the morning?' he enquired.

Tessa flung him a startled look. 'The fact that there's one every morning,' she retorted warily.

'Not in a force-eight gale, there isn't,' he derided. 'In fact, it amazes me you would even contemplate taking a boat in such nasty weather, given the almighty fuss you made over the mild squall we came over in.'

Tessa rummaged through her mind for something to say to hide her complete oblivion to the appalling deterioration in the weather. 'Well, anyway, I've still things to do,' she muttered defiantly. She actually had a hazy recollection of when the wind had started howling with such eerie intensity hours earlier, she realised dazedly, but she had been in such a state by then that even the roof caving in wouldn't have registered that deeply with her.

'Don't let me keep you from doing them, darling,' he murmured, his eyes dark with loathing.

'I shan't,' she replied, wondering at the flaw in her nature that could have led her to love a man who deserved only her contempt. 'I can't have my pigeons going hungry.'

'I'm afraid that's an English saying I'm not familiar with,' he retorted, his eyes narrowing as she turned and walked away.

'It's not a saying, *darling*,' she hissed over her shoulder. 'There's no telephone here and I certainly wouldn't want Mrs Maguire listening over my shoulder while I spoke to my gutter press cronies—so it stands to reason I must have a flock of pigeons at my disposal.'

Her satisfaction in having had the last word had died in her even before she reached the sitting-room. Suddenly the very idea that she had ever once even considered herself capable of earning a living by words struck her as pathetically ludicrous. Whether written or spoken, she had never been skilled with words, she reminded herself harshly; when the going got tough they invariably deserted her—the fact that for once they hadn't was simply the exception that proved the rule!

Terrified by the realisation of how close she was to breaking-point as she collapsed in a trembling heap on the sofa, she made no attempt to hold back the anger burning so savagely within her—it was the only prop she had holding her together.

But she wasn't too sure how firm a prop her anger would be as she found her mind dodging around the minefield of memories it must avoid at all costs. And she felt something within the core of her shrivel with despair when she couldn't avoid thinking of how he had so recently denied loving Angelica...and how he hadn't even bothered to attempt to make any such denial while he was making his horrifying accusations.

And to think that she had actually felt a twinge of guilt over not having had a chance to admit the naïve plans she had once had to write a clandestine article on him, she reminisced bitterly. A shiver of pain sneaked through her as she remembered the cloud of delusion on which she had still been floating when, earlier that morning, she had experienced that unwarranted pang of guilt…and to think she had actually planned to tell him all about it the moment he came back, she thought with a shudder of disbelief. Yet now it was almost like a macabre sort of poetic justice at work, she mused distractedly; her putative journalistic ambitions had been more a mixed-up means of getting back at poor Charles than any genuine yearning to write—yet now she was being accused of participating in a form of journalism for which she felt nothing but revulsion.

She stiffened at the sound of a knock on the front door, then relaxed a fraction when she realised that it would be Sean's wife with the evening meal. But a feeling of panic washed over her several minutes later when the sound of voices came to her from the hall and was instantly drowned out by the rising pitch of the wind as it screeched with renewed vigour round the contours of the house.

'That was Mrs Sweeny with our supper,' announced Sandro, the door slamming shut behind him as he strolled to the fire and stood before it with his back to her. 'And Sean with provisions. It seems the entire island is about to batten down against the weather, so we'll be fending for ourselves till it blows over… God knows how long that will be; Sean's brought us enough to last a siege.'

The sense of being trapped almost suffocating her, Tessa leapt to her feet, her only thought the sanctuary of her room as she stumbled towards the door.

'No, Tessa…wait!' he called out as he turned.

'Wait for what?' she demanded bitterly, the glitter of tears in her eyes as she spun round. 'More accusations, or more of your scintillating comments on the weather?'

'Damn it, Tessa,' he exploded, 'if you had nothing to do with those bloody articles, why don't you just say so?'

'Say so? My word against your precious Angelica's? I wouldn't waste my breath!'

'Stop calling her my precious Angelica,' he rasped. 'And anyway, she didn't want to believe it was you; she... Oh, God!' he groaned, shaking his head angrily and muttering under his breath in Italian.

It was the heart-churning memory of the teasing laughter in his voice the last time she had heard him speak that language that brought an involuntary sob choking from her as she turned and fled.

He caught up with her in the hall, stepping in front of her and barring her flight with his body.

'Tessa, please...you just don't understand,' he protested, reaching out and cradling her against him as harsh sobs racked her body. 'I tried to trust you...I didn't want to hurt you like this.'

'You *haven't* hurt me!' she lied fiercely, tearing herself free. 'It's not hurt reducing me to this, it's...it's anger and complete disgust!'

'Disgust?' he echoed in stunned protest. 'Tessa, not because we made love...?'

'Why not?' she choked, shaking her head as though by doing so she could blot out the words.

'Because that was your first time and—'

'It wasn't!' she screamed, the need to silence him dragging the lying denial from her. But it was the look of bemusement that flickered momentarily across his face that told her she had succeeded in planting a tiny seed of uncertainty in him—and that imbued her with a perverse strength. 'I can't think what gave you that ridiculous idea,' she added almost gloatingly. 'Anyway, my disgust is directed solely at you. You were quite happy to deny your love for Angelica when you wanted to get me into your bed, but, more than that, it's the way you stooped to taking your guilt out on me once you'd got what you wanted that really disgusts me.'

'My God, Tessa—'

'And you didn't really believe I had a hand in those articles, did you, Sandro?' she continued ruthlessly, her pride goading her on. 'It was merely a convenient way for you to—' She broke off with a shriek of fright as he grasped her by the shoulders and virtually hauled her through to the kitchen. His fingers bit painfully into her flesh as he forced her down on to a chair and held her there.

'If you think you can—'

'Shut up and damned well listen!' he roared through her protests. 'I've already told you I'm not in love with Angelica—because I *don't* love her, *not* because I desire you! And if I were in love with her, or any other woman, for that matter, I'd not have been here with you in the first place, let alone have made love to you—have I made myself clear?'

Tessa glared up into his blazing eyes, hating herself for the riotous effect his words were having on her heart.

He released her abruptly, dragging his hands wearily over his face. 'Perhaps I'm beginning to have a few ideas as to who the culprit behind those articles might be,' he sighed. 'But surely their very existence gives you some sort of understanding of why I have problems trusting people?'

'I understand only too well!' exclaimed Tessa bitterly

as her heart for once paid heed to her cautioning mind. 'You're prepared to sleep with me, but not to trust me!'

'Tessa, that's not what I meant,' he groaned. 'I'm sorry—I'm asking too much in expecting you to understand.'

'What you mean is that you don't trust me enough to explain,' stated Tessa quietly, the memory of Angelica's unwelcome confidences hovering like malevolent spectres once more in her mind. She found it impossible to doubt his word that he didn't love Angelica: apart from that terrible time today, she had always instinctively known that he didn't. But there was something between the two of them that she couldn't begin to fathom—and which he was not prepared to divulge…and for that reason, and despite the undiminished love she still bore him, she could trust him no more than he could her.

'Perhaps it's not quite as simple as it seems to you,' he stated quietly. 'But when I said I would turn over a new leaf, I honestly did try.'

'I know you did.' She sighed, the fact that they were reduced to conversing in what virtually amounted to a ritualised code doing nothing to alleviate the sensation of bleak weariness that had settled chillingly over her.

'But any attempt at trust has to be a two-way thing…and I have a strong feeling there's something you feel you must hide from me.'

Of course there was something she had to hide from him, she thought wearily, now more than ever; the last thing she wanted him to know was that she had made the mistake of falling irrevocably in love with him. Even if he didn't laugh in her face at the very idea of it, there was no knowing if or when Angelica might again pick up the telephone and make him dance to whatever tune she chose to play. And that was what had happened, she told herself bitterly: Angelica had played and Sandro, however briefly, had danced.

'Oh, dear,' he murmured with a theatrical sigh, then moved behind her chair and placed his hands lightly on her shoulders. 'And there I was hoping you'd convince me my instincts were all wrong.' In the instant she was turning to look up at him, his hands began sliding seductively down from her shoulders towards her breasts. 'Tessa—'

'No!' she cried, horrified by the fire of need searing through her as she twisted free of his touch. 'Sandro, how *dare* you? Only minutes ago you were hurling names and accusations at me—'

'Tessa, I'm sorry,' he groaned, stepping back. 'My timing was absolutely lousy…it's just that when I touched you—' He broke off with a shrug, then dragged his fingers agitatedly through his hair. 'But as for what I put you through earlier—Tessa, I've told you I'm sorry.' He squatted down beside her, gazing up at her from wary, troubled eyes. 'Tessa, I really am.'

'Oh, that's terrific,' she grated, completely thrown by the arousing effect his proximity was having on her. 'You're sorry, so now I'm expected to leap into your arms. What sort of fool do you take me for?'

'I don't take you for any sort of fool…what I see is a woman who, despite her wholly justifiable anger, still wants me as I want her.' He placed his bandaged hand on her knee to stop her as she made to rise. 'Tessa, please…I'm prepared to accept you just as you are— why can't you do the same with me?'

She gazed down at the dazzling white of the strapping on his tanned hand, conscious of again decoding his words and wondering what it could be in his make-up that made him so preoccupied by the fact that she was hiding something from him. She also wondered what it was about him that made him so blind to what it was—surely her actions last night had told him more than any words ever could.

'How many stitches did the doctor put in your hand?' she asked, not caring how glaringly obvious her avoidance of answering his question must be.

'OK—if you want to change the subject, we'll change it,' he murmured ruefully. 'I've no idea.'

'He taped it up very neatly,' she said, reaching out a finger and timidly stroking it against the material, while every muscle in her ached to throw her arms around him.

'I preferred the way you did it,' he said, the husky softness in his voice causing her to snatch back her hand. 'Don't worry, Tessa,' he teased, smiling as he straightened. 'I'm not trying to seduce you...not right now, that is.'

CHAPTER EIGHT

WHATEVER Sandro might have said, he had no intention of leaving well alone, thought Tessa frustratedly as she pottered around the kitchen preparing their evening meal—the first real meal she would cook for them and, she prayed, the last.

The trouble with Sandro was that it simply wasn't in his nature to leave well alone, especially not once he had decided something was being kept from him. Though boredom probably played a part in his irritating behaviour, she rationalised as she added stock to the casserole she had prepared, which amounted to his niggling away at her like a malevolent child let loose with a drill. His was also a temperament that didn't take kindly to sitting around doing nothing, something she had discovered to her cost that morning when she had been entering the remainder of her work on the word processor.

She popped the casserole in the oven and began tidying up, savouring the peaceful silence. Silence had been in exceedingly short supply that morning when she had been trying to work, she remembered wryly; she had lost count of the number of times he had interrupted her—invariably bearing coffee, the making of which, she strongly suspected, was the sole culinary skill he had mastered.

'It doesn't seem right,' he had strolled in and announced at one point. 'We're lovers, yet—'

'Sandro!' she had groaned in exasperation, even her

unreliable heart for once not bothering to respond with its customary abandonment at the mere sight of him—despite its lurching response to the words she had cut short.

'For heaven's sake, all I was going to say was that I know nothing about you,' he had protested glibly. 'I want to hear all about you.'

She had flashed him a withering look and attempted to get on with her work.

'I realise I haven't been all that forthcoming about myself,' he had continued relentlessly. 'Perhaps it would make it easier for you if I told you all about me first.'

There had been a look of paradoxically evil innocence on his face as he had proceeded to regale her with tales of his childhood—a string of the most outrageous lies she had ever heard.

'Tessa!'

He was having a bath, for heaven's sake, she told herself exasperatedly; the least she had hoped for was an hour of peace and quiet in which to prepare the meal.

A look of stubborn determination on her face, she began drying the utensils she had just washed.

'Tessa!'

She froze, panicking suddenly as she remembered what he had managed to do to his hand. It could have been a genuine bellow of pain, she thought, her heart pounding as she raced up the stairs, trying desperately to stop her vivid imagination from speculating on what he might have done this time.

'Sandro!' she called out when she reached the bathroom door. 'Are you all right?'

Silence.

'Sandro!' She hammered on the door then, with a groan of terror, flung it open and rushed in.

'This bloody thing's driving me insane,' came his languid voice from the bath.

Unable to catch her breath for the thunderous pounding of her heart, Tessa's eyes widened in outraged disbelief as Sandro stretched out a hand to her over the side of the bath, a look of scowling irritation on his face as he gazed down at the sodden dressing covering it.

'For God's sake, Sandro, why didn't you answer me?' shrieked Tessa, once she had her wind back. 'I thought you'd drowned or something!'

'It's a good job I wasn't drowning—the time it took you to get here,' he muttered morosely, then glanced over at her with a cherubic smile. 'But now that you're here you can wash the bits I can't reach with my right hand.'

'I can what?' croaked Tessa, murder in her heart. 'My God, I don't believe this! If you think—'

'If you're going to make such a production out of it, forget it,' he muttered, then rose and stepped nonchalantly from the bath. 'Well, it's pointless my lying in there catching my death of cold when you're too heartless to help... Damn it, where's the towel?'

Tessa took the bath-towel from the rail beside her and flung it at him, and, finding her eyes resisting her every attempt to avert them, began dazedly wondering if she actually was gawping at that naked, glistening and altogether magnificent body quite as avidly as she felt she must be.

'Would it be too much to ask you to have a look at this?' he muttered, plainly not in the least self-conscious about his nakedness as he slung the towel over one shoulder and approached her with his sodden, bandaged hand outstretched. 'It's stinging—though I suppose that's the effect of dipping it in soapy water.'

'You're not supposed to get it wet,' said Tessa, her voice strained. She simply couldn't believe the electrifying effect his nakedness was having on her.

'I know I'm not,' he retorted irritably. 'It just happened.'

'You'd better get dressed and come downstairs,' muttered Tessa, 'and I'll change the dressing.'

'OK, but remove this one first—it's killing me.'

Tessa hesitated, torn as to what to do. He seemed totally engrossed in his hand…but something told her he was perfectly aware of the electrifying effect he was having on her.

'What's wrong, Tessa?' he mocked softly, confirming her every suspicion. 'It's not as though you haven't seen me like this before.'

She turned her face aside as she felt the heat rise in her cheeks.

'If we had been bathing together, as we should have been, I wouldn't have got my hand into this mess,' he whispered seductively. 'You can't expect me to pretend last night never happened,' he said, drawing her towards him. 'Last night did happen and I want you more than ever because of it.'

She could feel the damp heat of his body permeating her clothing as his mouth opened hungrily on hers, and the swift surge of his physical arousal like a flaming sword, igniting a searing pain of hunger in the depths of her being.

She tore herself from his arms, racing blindly until she reached the sanctuary of the kitchen. When she finally halted beside the table, she placed both her hands on it, leaning down heavily on them for support while her starved lungs gasped for air as though recovering from a gruelling marathon. And even as she stood there, listening to her own tortured breathing, she wondered where she had found the strength to deny herself what every nerve in her body still clamoured for.

It was twenty minutes before he appeared—time enough for her to have achieved an outward semblance of calm and for the stomach-churning urgency of the need in her to have subsided to an aching dullness.

'Mm, something smells good,' he announced with the brightness of a casual visitor as he sauntered in, his hair gleaming with dampness and black as the tracksuit he now wore.

'It's only a casserole—it won't be ready for a while yet,' she muttered, the violence of the need once again leaping in her deciding her that being in love with him was bad enough without her having to contend with this positively unnatural sexual appetite he seemed to have awoken in her. 'I'd better see to your hand.'

'It's OK—it's practically dry,' he said, picking up the kettle and starting to fill it. 'Coffee?'

'Sandro, that dressing has to be changed.'

He put down the kettle with a resigned shrug, then went to the table and sat down, a disturbingly speculative look in his eyes as he placed his damaged hand with its still sodden dressing on the table.

'That's another thing I didn't know about you,' he said, his eyes following her every movement as she got out the first-aid box. 'The fact that you can cook.'

Here we go again, she thought wearily, back to his niggling and needling away at her.

'Well, I hope you can cook too,' she stated briskly, taking the chair beside his and opening up the first-aid box, 'because if we're still stuck here tomorrow it'll be your turn to cook the supper.'

'Haven't you forgotten something?' he enquired when she reached for his hand.

'Don't worry, I'm sure your hand won't interfere with your cooking—I'll bind it up extra neatly, if you like.'

He again drew back his hand when she reached for it. 'You misunderstand me, Tessa,' he murmured, his eyes mocking. 'Your allergy…you haven't put on the gloves.'

'I…I shan't be using any antiseptic,' she stammered, the colour flaring in her cheeks. Once again, the problem of her own hands hadn't even crossed her mind!

'But you can't be too sure,' he murmured sweetly, digging in the box and passing her the pack of surgical gloves. 'You never know what the doctor might have used on that dressing—and some of it might rub off on you.'

Tessa slipped on a pair of the gloves, feeling no shred of gratitude for his having pointed out her omission— she strongly suspected that he had derived a perverse sort of pleasure from it.

'And as for my culinary duties, I can only cook porridge,' he murmured as she began removing the soaked dressing.

'Porridge?' exclaimed Tessa disbelievingly.

'Didn't I tell you I had a Scottish nanny?'

'A Scottish nanny doesn't quite fit in with those lurid tales of your childhood you were recounting this morning,' she responded drily.

'Lurid? I had a perfectly delightful childhood, even though it was like that of no other child. Though I suppose the time has come for me to move on to my adolescence—I do hope you've the stomach for it; it really is quite harrowing in parts… Ouch!'

'Sandro, would you please keep your hand still?'

protested Tessa, frowning as she examined the livid wound and the three garish stitches adorning it.

'Why are you frowning?' he demanded in alarm.

'Because I always frown when I'm concentrating. Stop being such a baby!'

'I can't help it,' he murmured as she began putting on a fresh dressing; 'I'm used to being pampered, and besides, I'm always tetchy when I'm frustrated... How does it affect you, Tessa—apart from making you forgetful?'

'I'm not forgetful!' she exclaimed indignantly.

'You forgot the gloves, didn't you?'

'Sandro, will you just shut up while I finish doing this?' she protested, and was appalled to see that her hands were once again shaking—something his eagle eyes had no doubt spotted long before she had!

'Tessa, why did you come here with me? In fact, why did you come to work on my film in the first place?'

'Sandro, let me finish this, will you?' she snapped, completely thrown by the sheer unexpectedness of his questions. She had come here because she had probably already been in love with him by then, she thought weakly; and, as for what had brought her to Ireland in the first place, she had no more intention of telling him that than she had of why she had stayed on!

He rose when she had finished, and without a word of thanks returned to making coffee.

'I know—let's talk about the weather,' he growled belligerently as she packed away the first-aid box. 'God knows how long we could be holed up here. But, unlike you, I haven't the time to sit around doing nothing for weeks on end.'

'Firstly, you're being ridiculous talking about it running into weeks,' snapped Tessa, her heart turning to lead at the very idea. 'And secondly, I don't know where you got the idea that I have time to waste.'

'You're here, aren't you?'

'Only because I had a few weeks to spare between jobs,' she lied, racking her brains in an effort to remember what, if anything, she had said to him about her work—or lack of it.

'Oh, so you actually do have a job, do you?'

'I happen to have a very fulfilling career, if you must know,' she lied on extravagantly, then wondered wretchedly when all this lying would ever stop. It was getting to the stage where every question he asked she either avoided answering—which only seemed to goad him to dig deeper—or she answered with a lie.

'And as this oh, so fulfilling career of yours is plainly connected with the Secret Service,' he snarled, 'I shan't embarrass you by asking for any details.'

'Why don't you just get out of here and leave me alone?' she shrieked as her temper snapped. 'Go out for a walk—and throw yourself over a cliff while you're at it!'

'It would solve far more problems if you simply came to bed with me,' he roared back at her. 'It isn't going to get any better, you know—any minute now we'll be at one another's throat!'

'Bed! Is that all you can think about?'

He slammed the coffee-jug down on to the table and marched over to her.

'Tell me, Tessa, what exactly have *you* been thinking about for most of the day?' he demanded, his eyes burning down into hers.

'Sandro, please...don't,' she pleaded, a strident voice inside her demanding to know why she was doing this to herself...why she was subjecting herself to this unnecessary torture when all she need do was hold out her arms to him.

'Damn it, Tessa, why can't you ever give a straight answer to a question?' he raged, then dragged her into his arms. 'No—don't fight me,' he protested softly. 'There's no need to, I promise. All I want is to hold you.' He buried his face in her hair. 'Tessa, wanting you like this is driving me crazy... I know I have the most appalling temper, but one thing guaranteed to make me fly off the handle is not knowing where I stand. Whatever you may think, deep down I have a very forgiving nature...there are few things I wouldn't forgive as long as I'm dealt with honestly.'

She was having considerable difficulty digesting those soft words pouring into her ear; she was too preoccupied trying to contain the longing melting through her like liquid fire. But eventually those words did get through to her, and brought an incredulous howl of protest from her.

'Those articles!' she raged, fighting without success to tear free from his hold. 'You still actually believe I had something to do with them! You—'

'No!' he groaned, swinging her off her feet as he hugged her suffocatingly to him. 'I don't think you had anything whatever to do with them!'

She gazed up at him in dazed bewilderment when he returned her to her feet and then released her.

'I'm nothing if not stubborn.' He sighed, stooping and placing a light kiss on her forehead. 'Which is why I'm turning over a new new leaf.'

'You're mad,' croaked Tessa, a love far more powerful than the searing desire she had just experienced now racking through her.

'Mad as a hatter,' he conceded with a chuckle, then took her by the hand and led her to the table.

'Shall we have that coffee now—or do you think it might spoil your appetite for that delicious-smelling supper?'

She shook her head, her expression totally bemused. 'I'd love a coffee.'

As mood swings went, she thought anxiously, this was certainly one of his better ones—but he did seem to have a disturbing amount of them.

He was fulsome in his praise of the meal, even though it was nothing more than a common-or-garden stew. But gradually the odd note of irritation had begun creeping into his voice and their attempts at light conversation had grown more and more stilted. And this time Tessa was prepared to take full blame. It was impossible to hold a relaxed conversation while constantly on guard against letting something slip, she reasoned dejectedly, still reeling from how close she had come to making a jocular reference to her stepfather's newspaper empire, and the clumsy ineptness with which she had stopped herself.

'I've decided I'd like to have another look at that cove along from the caves tomorrow, if humanly possible,' he announced as he entered the sitting-room with a tray of coffee.

Tessa, who had sat before the fire racking her brains for a safe topic of conversation to introduce, while he had been making the coffee, wondered if he hadn't been doing exactly the same as he smoothly launched into giving her a detailed account of the plot of the film he was to make on the island.

'Mind you,' he finished with a rueful chuckle, 'if what

I've heard about the summer weather here proves correct, we might as well do the whole shoot in black and white.'

'Have you ever made a film in black and white?' asked Tessa, at last beginning to relax.

'No, but it's a medium both Paolo and I find fascinating and are determined to try one day.'

'If that's the case, why don't you shoot this next one in black and white?'

'It's not quite as simple as that,' he laughed. 'For one thing, it wouldn't work for that particular film and, for another, black and white, unfortunately, is a medium that isn't regarded as commercially viable these days, though Paolo and I are convinced it could be, given exactly the right scenario…which is why we're biding our time.'

'If you know what you're looking for, I'm sure you won't have much difficulty finding it.'

He threw back his head and laughed. 'Neither of us has any hard and fast ideas as to what it is we're looking for, but our instincts will let us know when it turns up.'

'From what I've heard, films cost an absolute fortune to make,' said Tessa, his mention of instincts reminding her uncomfortably of her own depressingly powerful instincts that had warned her of the heartache she was already tasting. 'You must have great faith in your instincts,' she added wanly.

'They rarely let me down, so why shouldn't I?' he replied, a decided coolness entering his eyes. 'If you can't rely on your instincts, when all else fails, what can you rely on…or don't you agree, Tessa?'

'Yes…I suppose you're right,' she muttered, and wished it weren't so.

It had seemed so safe, she thought miserably, talking about films…yet look where it had led.

'My mother swears that by the time I was eight she knew I was destined to become involved with films—by then I'd become as addicted as my father to the old classics, which the two of us watched endlessly.'

'That's incredible!' exclaimed Tessa, so buoyed with relief by his diplomatic return to a safe topic that she launched herself into it with guileless abandon. 'My stepfather's the same. He has the most incredible collection of old films. I used to climb on his knee when I was tiny and watch them with him. I became almost as addicted as he is—which used to drive my mother mad, as she had an aversion to films that aren't in colour.'

'You have a stepfather?'

She froze, struggling to keep a hold on herself.

'Yes,' she said. She had a stepfather—so what? She didn't have to say who he was.

'His name—is it Morgan?'

Tessa shook her head. 'No, I...I use my real father's name.' Yet another lie! 'Why do you ask?'

'I just wondered whether or not you and Babs were blood cousins—I have tribes of them.'

'We are. My father was her uncle, but he died when I was very young.'

'That's sad—but you seem to get on very well with your stepfather.'

'I do. I love him as though he were my real father.' And she did, she reminded herself with a pang of remorse. They had their ups and downs, and probably always would—just like any other father and daughter.

'And so you should—the man who introduced you to cinema's greats!' he exclaimed with teasing indignation, then added, switching to a softness that sent a shiver of apprehension through her, 'Though I wonder what he has to say about all these terrible men his little girl gets involved with.'

Tessa reached for her cup and took a gulp of her now cold coffee.

'Tessa, you can hardly expect me to believe that your relationships with men are the disaster you claim them to be.'

'You can believe what you like,' she lashed out, feeling horribly cornered, 'but the truth is that, on the whole, I have pretty appalling taste in men.' She was beginning to make herself sound like some sort of half-wit where men were concerned, she thought incredulously.

'You really know how to flatter a man, darling,' he drawled, then grinned as he caught her startled look. 'In what way appalling, Tessa—are they married, or simply degenerates?'

'Of course they weren't married!' she exclaimed in horror.

'Oh, I see—just degenerates.'

'They were…they just weren't suitable.'

'In the same way I'm not suitable?' he mocked.

She flashed him a look of loathing, but said nothing.

'At least we appear to have one thing in common,' he murmured. 'Our problems with the opposite sex.'

'Oh, yes,' sneered Tessa as anger flared in her, 'it's common knowledge what a problem you have with women—their never giving you so much as a second glance, for example?'

'OK, so I don't have any trouble attracting the opposite sex,' he replied, without any apparent rancour, 'but then, neither do you.'

'What makes you so sure of that?'

'The fact that I have an extremely good eye in that respect—it comes in very handy in my line of work,' he replied smugly. 'There are some women who only have to walk into a room to start heads turning.' He leaned back, his eyes narrowing as they scrutinised her. 'You, of course, don't fall into that category.'

'Of course,' she muttered acidly. 'That's your category—for men, that is.'

He gave a throaty chuckle, but he didn't deny it. 'It's when men come face to face with you that things start hotting up.'

'Assuming, that is, that a head-turner hasn't just strolled by and taken the limelight,' murmured Tessa helpfully. 'But do continue; I love listening to experts.'

He grinned. 'You mustn't be offended when I tell you that, at first glance, most red-blooded men might find your looks a trifle too angelic for their tastes—'

'Angelic? Me?'

'I warned you not to take offence.'

'I haven't!'

'So why won't you let me finish?'

'Feel free.'

'All right—as I was saying, most red-blooded men might find your looks a trifle too angelic for their tastes, if it weren't for your completely contradictory mouth.'

'My mouth?' squeaked Tessa, then hastily clamped her hand over that offending organ when he flashed her an impatient look.

'You have an uncompromisingly voluptuous mouth which, together with your eyes, simply doesn't go with the rest of your face.'

'I don't need you to tell me I have a big mouth,' she retorted huffily. 'I've always known it's my worst feature...but what's wrong with my eyes?'

'Your mouth isn't your worst feature,' he replied in matter-of-fact tones; 'in fact, it ties with your eyes for being your best feature... I can't ever remember having seen eyes quite as delightfully dirty as yours.'

'I beg your pardon?' gasped Tessa, convinced she had misheard.

'They're dirty, Tessa,' he chuckled. 'Beautifully, magnificently and unashamedly sexily dirty—as is your mouth. My God, what a combination! So don't ever try kidding me you have any problems attracting men.'

Unable to come up with a single word, Tessa glowered at him in resentful silence—while her heart turned a series of somersaults.

'Tessa, most women would consider I'd just paid them quite a compliment.'

'Only the ones who don't mind being regarded as little more than sex objects,' she retorted, and knew it was one of the most hypocritical remarks she had ever made.

'One of your problems is that you haven't got what it takes mentally to handle the type of man you attract,' he informed her, an edge in his voice.

'Really—and what type of men are they?'

'Strong men, who tend to thrive on challenge,' he replied, 'and who are used to getting what they want.' His eyes swept slowly over her, bringing colour rushing hotly to her cheeks...had he really believed her crazy claim not to have been a virgin? 'Obviously there will be the odd wimp or two, drawn by that angelic quality in your looks...come to think of it, you'd be a lot safer going for one of them.'

'Would I really?' she snapped, a sickness of desolation washing over her. For a few brief hours she had actually nurtured the insane hope that he could love her...this man who was now casually suggesting the type of man to follow him!

'Yes, you would—*really*,' he drawled. 'But, unfortunately for you, it's not the wimps to whom you're drawn, is it, Tessa?'

'Why unfortunately?' she asked, leaping up and tending to the fire in an attempt to buy time in which to recover from the vicious blows being dealt her.

'Don't ask me—you're the one claiming to have the problems.'

'And you're the one claiming they're what we have in common,' she lashed out as she spun to face him. 'But what exactly is your problem, Sandro? You walk into a room and women are captivated—can't you handle that?'

'What was it about me that so captivated you, Tessa?' he snarled. 'My knock-out looks?'

The naked venom in his words sent a ripple of shock through her.

'Perhaps it was my renown as a director? Or could it have been my fabled background—my being the only son of a living legend?'

'You're not the only person with problems arising from having a famous parent,' she retorted. Though her stepfather's fame was nowhere in the league of that of the legendary Leona Carlotti, and though it had been something from which he had almost obsessively tried to protect both herself and Rupert, she none the less still smarted from the battering her ego had suffered on the couple of occasions men had tried using her as a means of gaining access to the powerful Charles Conway.

'So—who's your famous parent, then?' he demanded, his cold words cutting through her unpleasant reminiscences.

'Well, it's hardly—' She broke off, weak with shock at the realisation of what she had, once again, almost let slip. 'I...I was speaking generally, not particularly.'

'In other words, you haven't the slightest idea what you were talking about.'

Rattled by his sneering tone, hating him for the paranoia in him that made it impossible for her to reveal the identity of her stepfather and tortured by the love that refused to die in her, she rounded on him blindly.

'It must be such a drag being the handsome, talented son of a famous mother! Just think how wonderful it would be if you were a plain, down-and-out orphan, Sandro—you'd never have a single doubt as to whether or not you were loved for yourself!'

'Are you telling me you love me, Tessa?' he drawled, rising.

She turned and placed the fireguard in front of the fire. 'I'm going to bed,' she announced wearily, too drained even to bother attempting another lie.

'It doesn't matter how many leaves I try turning over,' he sighed, coming up behind her and resting his arms on her shoulders, linking them around her so that her chin rested on them. 'There are too many secrets between us for it to work.'

She nodded, probably the first honest thing she had done all evening, she thought disconsolately.

'Do you feel like braving the weather tomorrow to have another look at the cove?' he asked, his chin resting on her head. 'I think we could both do with a bit of fresh air—even if it does blow us away.'

As she again nodded, she was praying for him to turn her in his arms, to make love to her there and then. But something had already told her that he wouldn't, even before he released her and walked away, bidding her a soft goodnight.

CHAPTER NINE

SANDRO had been right, of course, thought Tessa as she gazed out across a sea seething in a raging turbulence of purples, greens and blues so dark in patches that they were almost black—they had both needed a blast of fresh air. And a blast it most certainly was, she decided as her slim body automatically braced itself against yet another capricious change in the direction of the wind— though it was now noticeably less ferocious than yesterday.

But there had been little in the way of calm in the atmosphere pervading the cottage, she reminded herself, a feeling of despair accompanying the inevitable quickening of her senses as her eyes followed Sandro's tall figure clambering over the rocks ahead.

There had been times during the night when only her pride had prevented her from getting up and going to him. But the heavy darkness circling his eyes that morning had told her that he had had as little sleep as she, and the almost palpable tension charging the air between them had also told her that the rejection her pride had so feared would never have materialised had she gone to him. Yet in his own implacable way he had rejected her last night, she reflected bemusedly; she had made no attempt to pull free from him when he had put his arms around her as they'd stood before the fire, and her every instinct had told her he had known she was his simply for the asking...and he had walked away.

'No—this place isn't right for what I had in mind,' he

called to her over the wind as he walked towards her. 'You're turning blue, Tessa,' he protested laughingly when he reached her side. 'It's time we got you home and into a hot bath. If you're good, I'll make you another bowl of porridge.'

'Much as I enjoyed it for breakfast,' responded Tessa, falling into step beside him, 'I don't really fancy porridge for my supper.' His serving them bowls of thick, perfectly prepared porridge had been the only light interlude in an otherwise nerve-racking morning. 'Did your nanny really teach you how to make it?'

'She did indeed.' He laughed, slipping an arm around her as a particularly vicious gust of wind sent her careering against him. 'But she wouldn't have approved of that sugar you ladled over yours—my nanny was a true Scot and allowed only salt on it.'

'Are you still in touch with her?' she asked, determined to prolong these fleetingly carefree moments for as long as she possibly could.

'Frequently. She married a doctor from Florence and together they've raised a brood of porridge-eating Florentines.' He halted suddenly and flung out his free arm in an expansive gesture. 'It would be a crime to film a place like this in black and white. Even in this filthy weather it's alive with the most glorious colour... Just look at it!'

Tessa gazed around her, across the neatly walled fields spilling down from the slopes of the cliffs, and saw a patchwork of colour that was indeed glorious—purples, browns and greens, here and there edged in a dazzle of gold where they sprawled untidily down to the sands. But as they trudged their way back to the cottage, in a silence that could almost have been described as companionable, she felt the coldness of an unendurable de-

spair enter her heart. Wretched though things were between them, it was the thought of never seeing him again
that filled her with such despair.

'It's amazing what a spot of fresh air can do!' he
exclaimed, the front door slamming shut behind them as
the wind snatched it from his grasp.

'"Fresh" isn't quite the word I'd have chosen to describe the air we've just been subjected to,' retorted
Tessa, but the strain already creeping into her voice
robbed her words of much of their intended humour.

'There goes my English letting me down again,' he
joked, then hesitated, his eyes suddenly darkening. 'But
I'm sure you know what I meant,' he added, an edge of
strain now detectable in his tone.

'Yes,' muttered Tessa, lowering her head and busying
herself with removing her wet jacket as her mind battled
to blank itself of its memories of that other time he had
joked about his non-existent problems with English.

'Tessa, I...'

She glanced up with questioning eyes as he fell silent,
and knew beyond doubt that they were sharing the same
memory.

'You'd better run along and have a bath,' he stated
brusquely, striding towards the kitchen as he shed his
own jacket.

There was a limit to how much of this emotional see-
sawing she could take, Tessa warned herself frustratedly
as she climbed the stairs. A short while ago the idea of
his soon being out of her life forever had had her wallowing in the depths of desolation; now she couldn't
wait to get back to London and on with sorting out her
life. She had no one but herself to blame for the ghastly
emotional mess she was in, she told herself harshly as
she ran her bath, but she owed it to her pride that when

she reached breaking-point, as she knew she soon must, it would be without him around to witness it... All she asked was for her strength and the weather to hold out for just a few hours more.

'I thought we could have bacon omelettes and chips,' announced Sandro when Tessa later joined him in the kitchen, 'but there isn't enough oil to make chips.'

'You could sauté the potatoes,' suggested Tessa, a little thrown by his apparent offer to cook. 'That wouldn't need much oil.'

'Perhaps you could see to that while I have a bath,' he muttered. 'I can only do chips.'

Relieved to be left on her own, Tessa had parboiled the potatoes and grilled the bacon ready for the omelettes by the time he reappeared.

'Good timing,' she murmured, going to the sink and rinsing her hands under the tap. 'It's all ready for you.'

'Where are you going?' he exclaimed in alarm as she walked towards the door.

'To laze in front of the fire while you finish off the supper.' After which she would take herself off to bed, she vowed silently, and that way ensure that she would survive the evening intact.

'But I told you I can only make chips.'

Tessa's eyes rolled with disbelief. 'For heaven's sake, Sandro, I've boiled and sliced the potatoes—all you have to do is fry them.'

'And the omelettes?'

'What about them? They were your suggestion.'

'I know they were, but I didn't say I could cook them,' he retorted irritably. 'Anyway, I thought I'd made it perfectly plain that I can't cook.'

'Since when have you ever made anything in the least

plain?' exploded Tessa, her frayed nerves threatening to snap completely—all she wanted was to be safely out of his company! 'First of all you say the only thing you can make is porridge, then you start talking about producing omelettes and chips! If you can cook the damned chips, as you now claim you can, you can't blame me for assuming you can also cook an omelette!'

'OK, I'll cook the bloody things,' he snapped, 'but don't blame me when they turn out inedible!' He flashed her a scowling look, then began cracking eggs with careless abandon into a bowl.

'Forget it, I'll do it,' seethed Tessa, marching to his side.

'No—I insist,' he growled malevolently, moving the bowl from her reach and cracking yet another egg, plus a liberal amount of its shell, into it.

'If you insist on doing something, I suggest it's the potatoes,' ground out Tessa as she elbowed him aside and grabbed the bowl. 'I can't stand shell in my omelettes!'

Still scowling blackly, he gave a shrug, then slammed a huge frying-pan down on the cooker, slung in the potatoes and sprinkled oil over them.

Biting back an exclamation of horror and mentally kicking herself for not having insisted on doing the lot on her own, Tessa occupied herself with removing every last trace of shell from the eggs, then began searching for an omelette-pan. All she found was an outsized pan capable of producing an omelette large enough to satisfy half a dozen hungry people. With no option but to make do, she took it to the cooker and was just in time to witness her co-chef apparently mashing her carefully prepared potatoes into the oil.

'What on earth do you think you're doing?' she groaned, this time unable to bite back a protest.

'Minding my own business,' he growled. 'What are you doing?'

Tessa flashed him a murderous look, but held her tongue as she threw a lump of butter into her pan, then drew it to one side of the cooker and gazed grim-faced into space.

'Well?' he demanded.

'Well what?' snapped Tessa. 'There's no point in my starting until the potatoes are almost done—and they'll take all night on that heat,' she added, reaching over and turning the heat up full blast under his pan.

What they eventually sat down to was an omelette with considerably less body than the average pancake and potatoes that, despite being charred black in parts, still retained an unpleasant element of underdone crispness.

'If ever I give up filming, and you the Secret Service, we could always open up a restaurant together,' he muttered as he removed the plates they had both pushed aside. 'I don't know about you, but I'm starving—fancy a bowl of porridge?'

Still seething inwardly, Tessa glanced up and found herself on the receiving end of a teasingly rueful grin.

'My God, that was ghastly,' she breathed, an answering smile creeping reluctantly to her face. 'But I've a better idea than porridge. You make the coffee while I wash up—then I'll butter us a mound of Mrs Sweeny's currant soda bread.'

Perhaps one day, in the dim, distant future, she would manage to appreciate the funny side of all this, thought Tessa as she did the washing-up, her ears tuned to every last nuance of the wind whistling round the cottage with ever-diminishing strength…but only in the very dim, very distant future.

'The wind's dying down, thank God!' exclaimed Sandro, helping himself to a slice of currant bread as Tessa poured them coffee in the sitting-room. 'With luck we should be on the mail boat in the morning.'

Tessa gave him an absent-minded nod as she handed him a cup, conscious of the complete illogicality of the resentment flaring in her at his words—all he had done was express a watered-down version of her own fervent prayers.

'I'm keeping my fingers crossed,' she stated, and wished she had managed to inject a little enthusiasm into the words.

'I suppose you are,' he said quietly. 'I haven't exactly made life easy for you while we've been here.'

'No, you haven't,' she replied breezily, a vice tightening around her chest, 'but this currant bread more than makes up for you—it's delicious.'

Once she had finished her coffee she would go to bed, then all she had to do was get through tomorrow's journey from the island back to Rathmullan, she promised herself almost cajolingly, and then she would be on her way to freedom…freedom to go to pieces with a vengeance, she acknowledged with a cynicism born of complete despair, while bitterness rose like bile in her throat.

'It is delicious,' he agreed, but there was an aggressive edge to his tone, 'though I'm afraid it doesn't do for me what it does for you.'

'Poor you,' retorted Tessa, returning her half-eaten slice of bread to her plate, certain that another mouthful would choke her.

'Yes, poor me,' he drawled, 'but I dare say I've only myself to blame. I've already told you how heavily I rely on my instincts when I've nothing else to go on. Take Angelica, for instance; I—'

'No, *you* take Angelica!' exploded Tessa. 'I haven't the slightest interest in the mysteries of your convoluted relationship with Angelica!'

She wanted to leap up and dash from the room, but doubted if her legs would support her; instead she picked up her coffee-cup, gripping it with both her badly shaking hands as she drained it.

'Do you really expect me to believe that?'

'No,' she said, rising to her feet despite her doubts about her legs. 'Why should you believe a word I've said when all I've ever told you is a string of lies?' she demanded, her stomach constricting sickeningly as she realised the element of truth in her distracted claim.

'Why the hell won't you simply tell me the truth?' he bellowed, anger blazing in his eyes as he rose and towered over her.

'You just can't leave well alone, can you, Sandro?' she exclaimed with bitter weariness. 'Why should there be one rule for you and a completely different one for me? The fact is that I'm no more prepared to be honest with you than you are with me!'

'It doesn't seem to have occurred to you that one could be dependent on the other!'

'That's precisely what doesn't seem to have occurred to you!' blazed Tessa, pushing her way past him.

'That's right,' he sneered, making no attempt to follow her; 'make your grand exit. I've already told you that sort of stunt doesn't work with me!'

She didn't care that she was almost blinded by tears as she stumbled her way to her room; all that mattered was that she had managed to escape before making a complete spectacle of herself. But it was fury with herself that throbbed through her as she tore off her clothes and got into her nightdress. She had known all evening how close she was to breaking-point and had kept warning herself about it; she knew how completely unpredictable he could be, yet still she had blithely left herself wide open to potential disaster!

She flung herself into the bed, burying her face against a pillow to stifle the harsh sobs racking through her slim body and chanting silently to herself that the weather would hold out and that by tomorrow evening she would be back in London.

'Tessa.'

'Go away!' she shrieked into the pillow, then felt her body tense unbearably as the mattress took the weight of his.

'Tessa, I never meant things to turn out like this,' he protested huskily, his hand reaching out and stroking gently against her hair. 'I may appear unforgiving, but I promise you I'm not.'

'How magnanimous of you!' she choked indignantly, twisting her head in a vain attempt to escape the hypnotic ministrations of his hand. He would, no doubt, be thrilled to bits to discover she had fallen in love with him, she recriminated bitterly with herself, especially when he had gone out of his way to be so obnoxious that no sane woman would have dreamt of loving him; and he really would be over the moon to hear of her erstwhile journalistic ambitions!

'Tessa, surely I've convinced you by now that I'm not in love with Angelica. The trouble is that I understand her far better than I do you and because of that—'

'I don't want to hear about her!' she howled. 'All I want is to get away from here—from you… I want to go home!'

'Don't worry, we'll both be in our respective homes by tomorrow evening,' he promised grimly, his hand dropping from her head, 'even if I have to steal a boat and row us over to the mainland to ensure it.'

'You can count on me to do my share of the rowing,' vowed Tessa. 'So you can—'

'Tessa, why are you crying?'

'I'm not.'

'OK, perhaps you're not right now,' he conceded impatiently, 'but you were.'

'I've found it bad enough being on the receiving end of your disgusting temper and paranoid suspicions for days on end,' she exploded bitterly, 'but it's the last straw when you won't even leave me in peace in my own room! Is it any wonder I'm reduced to tears?'

'One of the many things I find particularly amazing about you is the almost infantile guilelessness of some of your lies,' he drawled. 'Take that last one, for instance—you were crying before I came in here, and it therefore follows that my presence here can't logically be the cause of your tears.'

'If my lies are such a doddle to detect, why don't you go and get yourself a lamp?' she demanded distractedly. 'One with a really bright bulb in it. Then you could cross-examine me to your heart's content!'

'The whole point is that I'd rather you told me what I need to know,' he retorted wearily, 'without my having to resort to any such tactic.'

Tessa twisted herself upright, taking a deep breath in an effort to clear her head as she turned to face him. She almost choked on the breath she had just taken when she discovered him stretched out on the bed beside her, his shoulders propped against the bed-rest.

'Let me get this straight,' she gasped unsteadily. 'You

want me to answer a question you're not prepared to ask me…and it's down to me to divine what the question is?'

'I'm sure you won't have too much difficulty working it out,' he murmured softly.

Her first reaction was one of fear—fear that he actually might be mentally unbalanced; her second was of anger, pure and simple.

'OK, Sandro, you win—I fed the story about you and Angelica to the Press. Happy?'

'Try again, darling,' he drawled. 'I'm ninety-nine per cent certain you didn't.'

She wasn't certain why his reply should upset her so much, nor why it should start up the train of thought it did within her. Often, when she had been particularly angry, she had questioned his sanity; yet now she found herself questioning it in stomach-churning fear. She hadn't found it in the least difficult to accept that there was something slightly unbalanced about Angelica…now she found herself wondering if something in connection with Umberto Bellini's accident could have unbalanced both his sister *and* his friend.

'Sandro, there isn't any point in our carrying on like this,' she pleaded. 'After tomorrow our paths will probably never cross again.' She would never know how she got those words out; all she knew was that, unbalanced or not, she would love him for the rest of her life.

'No, there probably isn't any point,' he sighed, then reached out for one of her hands and raised it to his lips.

Tessa made no attempt to free her hand, stunned by the overpowering intensity of the longing awoken in her by the soft pressure of his mouth.

'If I were a liar I would tell you that I wanted nothing

more than to sleep here beside you tonight,' he stated tonelessly.

'And if you weren't a liar?' she asked, barely able to form the words for the suffocating pounding of her heart that had driven her to abandoning all consideration of anything other than the immediate present.

'Tessa, I—' He broke off, his hand tightening compulsively around hers. 'I'd get in beside you under the bedclothes and—'

'What, with all your clothes on?' she demanded, an intoxication of relief coursing through her and washing away every last vestige of restraint.

'No—only after you'd removed them all from me,' he whispered unsteadily, sinking his fingers into her hair and drawing her towards him as he slid his head down on to the pillow. 'You have two good hands, whereas I only have one.'

His kiss startled her, his lips gently rebuffing the un-inhibited ardency of her response with the lightness of their exploration.

'Tessa, are you sure you know what you're doing?' he pleaded against her parted lips.

'I'm sure,' she choked, the ghost of reason urging her to push him away even as she clung to him to reinforce her own certainty.

'I could just try to lie here beside you, if that was what you wanted,' he whispered huskily. 'I dare say I'd eventually manage to fall into some sort of stu-por…given enough time.'

'You might, but I certainly wouldn't!' she exclaimed indignantly, and felt love bubbling riotously in her at the sound of his laughter.

'So why aren't you undressing me?' he demanded with mock-exasperation.

'I...because I'm not sure where to begin,' she stammered, her nerve for a moment failing her.

'I am,' he murmured, raising himself slightly. Before she realised what he was about to do, her nightdress had been slipped up and over her head and tossed aside. 'Now, that wasn't too difficult, was it?' he whispered, his voice catching in his throat as he reached out for her.

A laugh shivered from her as she ducked free of his hands and unzipped his tracksuit-top. But she was reduced to an exclamation of exasperation when he made no effort to assist her in her struggle to ease it down over his shoulders.

'You're not very skilled at this, are you?' he murmured complacently, sitting up and stripping himself free of the top. He sank back down, a hint of teasing in the luminous darkness of his eyes as they challenged her to make her next move.

'No...I'm not,' she agreed, her hands trembling as she gave in to an overwhelming need to run her fingers through the silky darkness of the hair on his chest. 'Sandro, I—' She broke off, a sharp cry of longing escaping her as his hands began sliding purposefully over her body.

'Yes—you what, Tessa?' he urged huskily.

She loved him, she cried out in silent anguish; and soon she would be bitterly regretting all those moments when her pride had kept her from his arms.

'Tessa?'

'I lied when I said that you weren't the first to make love to me,' she blurted out distractedly. 'There's no reason why you should believe me now, but—'

'I do believe you,' he whispered unsteadily. 'It was your lie I didn't believe...that's the trouble with my instincts—as I've already told you, they rarely let me down.'

'Trouble?' she choked, but already her body was leaping to pulsating life beneath the electrifying touch of his hands.

'Forget all that,' he groaned, drawing her down to him. 'Tessa, forget everything but us here and now.'

But there was an uncontrolled, almost savage edge to the intensity of their lovemaking that left them shattered and speechless long after its explosive force had spent itself. And it was the bruising to which her heart had been subjected, far more than that of her body, that lingered on in silent warning in Tessa as they lay drugged and entwined in one another's arms.

'Tessa, I'm sorry,' he whispered raggedly, when she had all but convinced herself that he must be asleep. 'It shouldn't have been like that...as though we were making war instead of love.'

She turned away from him in silence as his arms slackened. She had deluded herself into thinking that tonight would be a magical memory she could store away forever in her heart, but the drugged peace her body had temporarily found had been at a price her heart couldn't afford.

'No—please, Tessa, don't turn from me,' he protested hoarsely, turning her forcibly and wrapping his arms tightly around her. 'Are you as battered and bruised as I am?' he whispered, while his mouth nuzzled gently against the corner of hers.

She started, then relaxed against him. 'Probably,' she sighed. 'Which is only fair, considering I was as much to blame as you,' she added, the truth slipping from her as though of its own volition. His attempts at gentleness she had answered with aggression, as though a subconscious part of her had been trying to punish him for his inability to give her the love she so craved.

'No,' he protested, 'I'm the one at fault. I—'

'Is this going to turn into a fight?' she sighed, her arms encircling his neck as she felt a warm rush of love ease aside the harshness of her hurts.

'No,' he vowed huskily, sliding her up against him and burying his head against her breasts. 'This most certainly won't deteriorate into a fight.'

Her relieved laughter turned to a sharp cry of shock as a searing heat shot through her, then switched to a squeak of protest as he rolled her on to her back.

'Sandro—what are you doing?' she gasped.

'I'm going to make love to you,' he replied with a husky laugh, pushing aside her hands to allow his to embark on a nerve-rackingly erotic exploration of her now achingly aroused body.

'No!' she protested distractedly when his mouth and tongue joined forces with his marauding hands.

'Do you want me to stop?'

'No!' she groaned, even as she sank her fingers into his hair in an attempt to stop him, an attempt that deteriorated into a voluptuous caress.

It was dangerous; it was too much like being truly loved for her to cope with.

'No—you're torturing me!' she cried out, and it wasn't solely because she felt incapable of taking any more of the exquisite torture being inflicted on her.

'No—I'm making love to you.'

'Sandro...please!' she choked, tugging distractedly on his hair.

There were soft, unintelligible words pouring from him as he answered her plea, entering both her heart and her body with the hot thrust of his passion, and they were words too easily mistakable for a litany of love.

And later, when she held him cradled against her in sleep, she remembered the sound of those words and then the hope that had danced to life in her that first night she had spent in his arms, and there was the wetness of tears on her cheeks as she felt that hope flicker weakly once more and then die.

CHAPTER TEN

TESSA gazed out over the restless waters of Lough Swilly through the rain-spattered panes of her hotel-room window, an equal restlessness churning within her. Now that she was back in Rathmullan it was as though she had been away a lifetime and her mind was no longer capable of readjusting to what had once been familiar.

She wandered aimlessly over to the dressing-table, frowning as she glanced down at the toiletry items she had left behind and finding herself unable to remember acquiring a single one of them. She opened one of the drawers, seeking the sight of familiar possessions in the hope that it would snap her out of this perturbing sense of disorientation. It was her folder she spotted—lying on top of some underwear—and it brought a groan of frustration from her. It was a familiar sight all right, she thought disconsolately as she picked it up, but hardly one to instil any ease in her.

For several seconds she gazed down at the folder in her hand, then tossed it down on the dressing-table and returned to the window.

It all seemed so far away, so long ago; yet it had only been this morning that Sean had come banging on the cottage door at an ungodly hour with the news that the mail boat had arrived early and would be leaving in under an hour. And Sandro…she thought, her heart giving its inevitable lurch; never at his best in the mornings, today he had seemed wan and his demeanour oddly tentative. It was hardly surprising that they weren't their usual selves, she conjectured uneasily; apart from everything else, they had barely had enough time to collect their things together. It had all been one mad rush— while she had gone ahead to the quay, Sandro had stopped off to settle the account with Mrs Maguire…and had nearly missed the boat.

But even on the boat, when it had been impossible to hold a conversation over the noise of the engines, he had seemed abnormally preoccupied, she fretted, resting her head against the coldness of the glass, her shoulders sagging as she at last gave in to the voice of sanity within her that demanded to know when she intended to stop playing these ridiculous games with herself and face reality. And the reality was that it was over—finished; the odds had been stacked against her and she had lost.

She turned with a start as the door opened.

'I've just had Molly book our flights,' announced Sandro, closing the door behind him as he entered.

Her eyes locking on to the handsome face which, only hours before, had hovered above hers transformed by passion, Tessa felt her heart pound as though it would burst, and her mind tossed aside all pretence of accepting reality and began praying for a miracle.

'Tessa, we have to—' He broke off, his jaw clenching as his gaze dropped to the floor a few paces ahead of him.

Tessa's eyes followed his, her heart constricting sickeningly as her gaze alighted on the cuttings, spilling on to the floor from the folder she had moments before tossed aside. Like one in a trance, she watched him walk to the dressing-table and pick up the folder as though led by the trail of the cuttings spilling from it.

'Getting down to work already?' he enquired chillingly, while anger and loathing blazed in his eyes. 'You don't believe in wasting time, do you, Tessa? But you've so much to add to it now.'

'Sandro…please,' she croaked, her head spinning.

'Good old Angelica—at least I can be certain when she's telling the truth, and she was certainly telling me the truth about this,' he drawled. 'What a shame no one thought to warn you how compulsively nosy she can be.' He tossed the folder aside with a gesture of contempt, the rest of the cuttings fluttering to the floor. 'Well, you can't say I haven't done my part and given you the story you were so desperate to get.'

' "Story" being the operative word,' croaked Tessa dazedly, her mind battling to explain away what it found impossible to accept.

'Exactly—get it in the least wrong, darling, and I'll sue you through every court there is.' He began ostentatiously reading her notes, the bitterness in his laugh as he did so slicing through her like a knife. 'There's one thing that puzzles me,' he mused, in tones that were almost conversational. 'I know there are rags that print anything they can get their tacky hands on—but I thought that even they required a modicum of literacy from their hacks.'

'I…what?' choked Tessa, by now feeling physically sick.

'This drivel,' he rasped, casting a contemptuous look towards the folder, 'you surely don't call it writing? A child could do better!'

'There is a difference between draft notes and a finished article,' lashed out Tessa, the remnants of her pride charging to her defence, 'though with your alleged affliction you can't be expected to appreciate that!'

'Ah, my dyslexia,' he sneered. 'Fact or fantasy—

which is it? Afflicted or not, I happen to be someone who's forever ploughing through drafts pared down to the bone; but it doesn't take a genius to realise that someone incapable of stringing a sentence together in draft form isn't likely to be able to do so in any other form.'

Tessa took a slow, deep breath in an attempt to regroup her scattered senses. This was the man she loved; the man who, instead of confronting her, had toyed her along to the extent of making love to her while believing her to be spying on him...and hating her all the while!

'I don't claim to be the greatest of writers,' she informed him with the quiet fury of an irreparable hurt, 'but that's hardly a problem for the stepdaughter of Charles Conway... You have heard of Conway Press?'

'Yes, I have heard of it,' he replied grimly, 'but I've heard nothing that would lead me to believe it was run by the type of man who'd take kindly to the idea of a woman—any woman—turning herself into a whore for the sake of a story.' He turned and walked to the door. 'I'm leaving now, but a car will be here at four to take you to the airport.'

Babs Morgan shook her head in dismay. 'Tess, how could you have been so stupid?' she groaned. 'Even I knew you'd never actually write the damned thing—but to leave the wretched notes lying around for Angelica to see...!'

'I'm telling you all this for a reason!' exclaimed Tessa defensively, having just given her cousin a very much edited version of what had taken place in Ireland—and only because her conscience demanded it. 'And it's not so that you can remind me how stupid I am.'

'I'm sorry, love…heck, why didn't you tell me about it when I rang and asked if you'd flat-sit?' protested Babs, her expression troubled.

'Because I…look, Babs, the point is that Charles summoned me to his office last week—'

'Summoned! Heavens, things must be really bad between you if it's come to—'

'They're not!' exclaimed Tessa, anxiety stretching her nerves close to breaking-point. 'He didn't want Mum to hear what he had to tell me…in fact, he was very sweet considering I'm the one responsible for his receiving those abusive letters from Sandro and his lawyers. He—'

'Hang on!' Babs interrupted, her expression one of increasing alarm. 'Why would Sandro and his lawyers be writing to Charles?'

'I thought you'd realise I hadn't let Sandro know who my stepfather was simply for the sake of conversation,' retorted Tessa with edgy impatience.

Babs shook her head in horror. 'Tess, you didn't imply that Charles would help you get into print…yes, you did!' she groaned. 'I've known you make some dumb moves in your time, love, but this has to be the dumbest!'

'It still didn't give him the right to call me a whore!' burst out Tessa in an unguarded explosion of bitterness.

'He called you a what?' gasped Babs, her entire body tensing with disbelief.

'I…well, he said something to me in Italian,' stammered Tessa, almost sick with the realisation of what she had so stupidly let slip, 'and that's what it sounded like,' she finished lamely.

'So—what happened with Charles?' asked Babs, still plainly stunned.

'He simply handed me the two letters...once I'd read them I expected him to blow his top.'

'Which, of course, he didn't.'

'He put his arms round me and asked if I felt up to explaining...and said he felt he might in some way be responsible,' muttered Tessa, her eyes brimming with the memory. 'Babs, those letters...'

'Why would Charles think he was in any way responsible?' protested Babs.

'Because of his attitude to my wanting to go into journalism,' sighed Tessa. 'The only reason he was against it is because he knows I haven't the slightest talent as a writer...but he couldn't bring himself to tell me outright.'

'Because he felt you'd taken such a knock over the nursing,' sighed Babs. 'He's almost as daft as you are!'

'The truth is, I behaved like a grossly spoiled brat!' exclaimed Tessa. 'But could we please get to the point of this—those letters? In his, Sandro ranted on about how I abused family connections—and this is where it's going to affect you,' she choked, close to breaking-point. 'He even went as far as to demand to be informed of any other family names, so that in future he could ensure that no one remotely connected with me could get within a mile of him!' She glanced at Babs in dread of her cousin's reaction and was bewildered to find her laughing. 'For heaven's sake, Babs, if he puts the word out in the film industry, your company could be ruined!'

'Tess, can you honestly—and I do mean *honestly*—imagine Sandro ever stooping that low?'

Tessa hesitated, despair cutting savagely into her as she pictured that laughing, handsome face.

'No...I...I just don't know what to think,' she whispered brokenly. 'He sounded so...so bitter and vengeful in that letter. I knew from the start he had a thing about his privacy… Charles was right about my not having the slightest talent for writing…in my heart of hearts even I knew it. But even if I could write, I'd never have done that article…it's just that things got so complicated with Sandro it became impossible for me even to tell him I'd ever contemplated it… Babs, I never dreamed it would be as bad as it was.'

'And I never dreamed you'd fall in love with him,' sighed Babs, almost wringing her hands. 'Look, I might as well tell you—a couple of weeks ago, in fact about half an hour after I'd rung you to ask if you wanted to flat-sit, Sandro rang me…he wasn't his usual self and it took him some time to get around to asking me for your address, which I realised was the purpose of his call and which triggered off the old Morgan alarm system. The way I saw it, the two of you had spent several days together and there had to be some good reason for your not having given him your address then.'

'What did you say?' asked Tessa, her tone tense.

'I said you'd gone off somewhere on holiday… Tess, I tried ringing you straight after, but no one was in, and I was off to Hong Kong for that shoot first thing the next morning,' sighed Babs. 'If it had been to do with payment for the work you'd done, he'd have said so—but he didn't; he just let the subject drop in a way most unlike him.'

'He probably wanted an address so that he could get his lawyers on to me!' exclaimed Tessa bitterly. 'And you were right about it not being to do with my pay— Carlotti Productions sent me a cheque here, care of you.'

'But you haven't denied that you're in love with him,' stated Babs quietly.

Tessa froze. 'You know my ghastly taste in men,' she retorted with bitter dismissiveness.

'You exaggerate,' chided Babs. 'And Sandro doesn't belong in that category anyway. But, from what I've heard, you don't see him for dust when a woman he's not interested in is after him and, believe me, he'd have been perfectly aware of what was happening with you, yet he stayed around and let it happen. So he couldn't exactly be described as averse to the idea of your loving him.'

'Of course not—he wanted it to happen!' exploded Tessa bitterly. 'It was his way of punishing me!'

'Tess, that's a terrible thing to say!' gasped Babs. 'Whatever crazy misunderstandings there are between you, you've got to get them sorted out.'

'All I need is already sorted,' choked Tessa vehemently. 'I've learned a lesson I needed to learn a long time ago. You saw the selfish way I went to pieces when I had to give up nursing. I wallowed in my own misery and refused to face reality... I behaved just as pathetically over Sandro and—' She broke off, shaking her head as though to clear it of the madness that had once possessed her. 'But never again—I've learned my lesson. But I don't want to see him again—not for as long as I live.'

'Tess, love—'

'No! Oh, damn it—here we go again!' she howled. 'I can't stop this ridiculous blubbing—it's so humiliating!'

Babs made to say something, then shook her head in defeat, tears welling in her own eyes as she rushed over to comfort the broken girl so desperately trying to contain her anguish.

'Tess, I'm afraid I'm taking off again first thing in the morning,' she said eventually.

'Where to?' gulped Tessa, reaching for the box of tissues on the side-table. 'You've only just got back.'

'I've a few things to chase up concerning one of our jobs,' muttered Babs. 'I shouldn't be too long—but you will stay on till I get back, won't you?'

Tessa managed a wan smile through her snuffles. 'I'm not feeling up to Mum's loving scrutiny just yet,' she admitted sheepishly. 'But also the job I'm doing at the moment doesn't finish till the end of the week, so it would be handy staying on as it's just round the corner.'

'Good,' said Babs, rising. 'Now for some tea.'

'No, Mum, I haven't turned into a recluse,' protested Tessa, transferring the receiver to her other hand as she wedged herself more comfortably on the hall floor between the wall and the telephone table. 'I know I was terrible company when I got back from Ireland—that was pure exhaustion. The only reason I've stayed on here the whole time Babs has been away is because I'm temping just round the corner.' A job which, in fact, had just finished several days earlier than expected, she thought guiltily. 'Anyway, I'd love to come home for supper tomorrow... Hang on, I think that must be Babs back now!' she exclaimed, lifting her head to listen to the sound of a key scratching in the notoriously temperamental front-door lock. 'OK, Mum, if she hasn't anything planned, I'll bring her along as well...and I love you both too,' she murmured before replacing the receiver.

She ducked her head, cursing silently to herself as she prayed that the lock would play up long enough for her to compose herself after the disastrous effects of her mother's loving words.

'Well-timed,' she called out when the door finally

creaked open. 'That was your aunt Jane on the phone, inviting us both round to supper tomorrow.' Her momentary crisis safely behind her, she eased herself to her feet and turned to face Babs. 'I wasn't too sure... No!' she gasped, her legs turning to jelly.

'I'm sorry, I didn't mean to frighten you, Tessa,' said Sandro quietly.

Raincoated and rain-splashed, his tall, almost exotically alien figure filled the small hallway with a presence that swamped her with stifling sensations of love and consternation.

'Finding a virtual stranger in their hall would frighten most people,' she lashed out in aggressive confusion.

'I'm sorry you regard me as a virtual stranger,' he stated in oddly hollow tones. 'Babs gave me her keys, but perhaps I'd have been wiser to ring the bell,' he added vaguely, his eyes flickering around the hallway before settling with piercing intensity on Tessa.

Almost speechless with shock, all she could think of was what a sight she must look. For a moment her mind went blank as she tried to remember what it was she had thrown on after her bath—and wished it had remained a blank when she recalled it was the nightshirt Rupert had given her for Christmas—a baggy, navy blue creation, tastefully emblazoned with a huge, bright yellow teddy-bear.

'I...Babs didn't tell me you'd be coming,' she stammered. Day after terrible day she had battled to rid her thoughts of him—how dared he turn up now and destroy the fragile numbness with which she had surrounded herself?

'How remiss of her,' he stated, with no trace of humour either in his tone or in the remorseless, gold-flecked brown of his eyes. 'But now that I'm here, is there any chance of my being offered a coffee?'

Tessa froze, praying it wouldn't happen even as she felt herself begin to disintegrate.

'No! There's no chance at all!' she choked as she turned and fled.

'This shouldn't take long,' he stated, following her into the living-room. 'But I've come a long way to say what I have to—and I intend saying it.'

Scrabbling upright on the sofa on to which she had hurled herself, Tessa watched in numbed silence as he made his way over to the bentwood rocking-chair and sat down. She saw the faint look of alarm that crossed his face when the chair rocked beneath his weight, and felt her own body slump back against the sofa when he began speaking again.

'I might as well start with Umberto Bellini. He's a man I respect highly, both professionally and as a friend.'

As she gazed over in dazed incomprehension at that rain-coated, rocking figure, she found herself wondering impatiently at her bemused reaction—wasn't it the state to which he had always reduced her?

'Umberto went through months of physical hell after his accident, which is why I was prepared to go to any lengths to protect him from anything that might add to the mental hell he undoubtedly suffered... He must, at times, have come close to giving up hope of ever walking again.'

She found it impossible to close her mind to what he was saying, listening trance-like to each word uttered in those achingly familiar accents while her eyes drank in every last detail of those finely chiselled features. There was the dark trace of a beard on his face and a drawn, unfamiliar look around his eyes that troubled her deeply.

At first she resented how much she cared, and the desperate longing that filled her to go to him and to feel the strength of his arms around her as she offered the comfort of hers. But the resentment gradually faded till all she was left with was the naked desperation of a love beyond her control.

'I'd never met Umberto's sister, Angelica, until the accident,' he continued in those same, almost detached tones. 'About a month later, a sound man Paolo had once worked with came to visit Umberto at the hospital and afterwards made a particular point of warning us that Angelica was one of those women with a tendency towards disturbing fixations on certain men. Paolo and I had never heard of such a thing before, but I immediately understood exactly what he was saying…but by then it was far too late.'

Tessa almost cried out aloud as a thousand different pieces seemed to click into place in her mind. 'I think there's actually a name for it,' she whispered dazedly. How she could have been so blind?

'Whatever it's called, being on the receiving end of it is a nightmare,' muttered Sandro. 'I was terrified in case the Press got hold of it and it got back to Umberto. In the end it got so bad that a relative of mine—a distant cousin on my father's side—suggested she and I pretend to be engaged. Carol and I have been close since we were kids—she was convinced it would put Angelica off…but it didn't, of course.'

'So your cousin broke off the engagement,' stated Tessa, trying desperately to rid her mind of the innuendo-filled article she had read.

'During that period, Carol and a close friend of mine

fell in love and are soon to marry. It was he who eventually told me how Angelica had been harassing Carol—not openly, but in a subtle, wearing way... So naturally I had the engagement called off in Carol's name.'

Tessa's head was spinning with the memories of the similar treatment she had experienced at Angelica's hands. Everything fitted so neatly into place that there was no shred of doubt in her that it was the truth, but a truth so bizarre that it was little wonder it had never crossed her mind. But, with no inkling of the truth to protect her, she had been confused to the point of questioning her own sanity, she reminded herself with mounting bitterness. And, shocked as she was by his disclosures, it in no way altered what he had done to her...nothing could ever alter that!

'I...I feel very sorry for Angelica,' she muttered as she tried desperately to stem the bitterness now washing over her like a tidal wave.

'The implication being that you think I don't,' he stated harshly. 'The crazy thing is that I could have stopped it right away if I hadn't felt so inhibited by Umberto's accident!' he exclaimed bitterly. 'I saw him a couple of days ago and he's one hundred per cent fit again—has been for some time now.'

Tessa gave him a startled look; Angelica had always made it sound as though her brother still had some way to go before full recovery.

'When I told him the whole sorry tale, the poor guy didn't know whether to laugh or cry.'

'He knew about Angelica's problem?'

'Yes. It's happened twice before—the first time when she was seventeen and their father died, the second five or six years later when a close friend of hers was mugged and badly hurt.'

'And the third after Umberto's accident,' whispered Tessa with an uncomfortable shiver.

'Yes, and the irony is that Umberto's the one person who can snap her out of it. It seems he couldn't stand the first guy she latched on to, and when he found out and told her so she dropped her victim like a hot potato. The second she picked on was a friend of his and it was only after weeks of trying to reason with her that he hit on the idea of claiming he didn't really like the poor guy anyway—it worked like a charm.'

'And he thinks it will for you?'

'He's certain it will.'

'But he and Paolo are the only two cinematographers you work with!' exclaimed Tessa, drawn into the conversation despite herself. 'How can he convince his sister he dislikes you and continue working with you?'

'Umberto will manage somehow, you can bet on it,' he replied. 'Angelica normally lives in the States anyway, but should he and I ever run into her when we're working together I'll produce a performance worthy of an Oscar to make sure she doesn't start having doubts.'

Tessa felt another savage wave of bitterness wash over her as she remembered some of the performances he had put on for her benefit.

'It must be very satisfying having a weight like that off your mind. But is there any particular reason for your telling me all this?' she demanded, pain and resentment spilling over into her words. 'Or did you simply have time to kill on the business that's brought you to London?'

'Ah—the reason for my telling you all this,' he drawled, stretching his legs out in front of him, his elegantly shod feet sliding in rhythmic silence against the carpet as he rocked the chair. 'I could hardly tell you before…knowing you were involved with the Press.'

'You knew nothing!'

'Because you told me nothing!'

Tessa shook her head in stunned disbelief—why hadn't he simply asked? 'All right,' she conceded wearily, knowing it was now far too late for the truth ever to be believed, 'I can't blame you for not telling me the truth about your relationship with Angelica…and I apologise.' She rose to her feet. 'Now, if you don't mind—'

'But what about my relationship with you, Tessa?' he asked tonelessly. 'I'm curious to hear your opinion of a man who would take advantage of his suspicion that a woman was falling in love with him…a man who would encourage her to do so because he wanted the power to hurt her as no other man could.'

She heard her own ragged intake of breath as she discovered that knowing in her heart of hearts how cynically she had been used was one thing, but that having it spelled out with such callous candour by the man who had so used her was another entirely.

'You're curious as to my opinion?' she echoed in a voice threatening to break. '*Curious*?'

'Hell, no—not curious, Tessa,' he groaned, rising and approaching her. 'I'm just chucking around words while I search for the right ones to beg your forgiveness for the unspeakable way I've treated you—!' He broke off with a muttered oath. 'Tessa, I'm having this difficulty finding the words because there's still part of me that refuses to accept how low I sank. It became a crazy point of honour with me that I didn't ask you for the truth—'

'Why…why?' she cried out distractedly.

'God only knows,' he groaned. 'There was a perverseness in me that demanded it came from you.' He reached out, grasping her hands in his in a gesture of pleading. 'Please, Tessa…I know I haven't the right to ask, but can you ever forgive me?'

She closed her eyes, the touch of his hands an aching, pulsating vibrancy throbbing its way throughout her body while the memories paraded their way through her mind.

'Of course I forgive you,' she whispered defeatedly. 'How could I not when you've had so much to contend with? You were prepared to do anything to protect Umberto…and I've only myself to blame that you saw me as a threat.'

'Tessa, no!' he protested, his hands tightening so fiercely on hers that she cried out. 'I'm sorry!' he gasped, releasing her. 'I didn't mean to hurt you.'

'I know you didn't…it doesn't matter,' she muttered with brittle edginess.

'But it does,' he insisted. 'I—' He broke off, flinging up his hands in exasperation. 'This is crazy,' he muttered. 'It's as though we were strangers…Tessa, this is all wrong!'

And it was all wrong, she thought wretchedly, a faint stirring of something like hope fluttering in her as her mind at last began to clear. She had loved and lost, but what was tearing her apart was the savage bitterness distorting her inevitable pain. But now she knew that things had never truly been as bad as they had once appeared, that only stubborn pride and ignorance of the facts on both their parts had led to the creation of that destructive bitterness… She could hardly blame him if he rejected the truth, but she knew he had to hear it.

'I think it's about time I made that coffee,' she stated, with a calmness that reinforced those faint stirrings of hope. And then she would have her say and pray that this time they could part with the air between them cleared of that terrible taint of misunderstanding.

Her obvious surprise, when she found him behind her in the small kitchen, brought a smile of boyish diffidence from him that tore straight into her heart. And there was that same, heart-wrenching diffidence in his attempts to make himself useful as she prepared the coffee that, even with the bitterness now gone, filled her with a choking awareness of the agony of the future yet to be faced.

What meagre hopes she had left were centred on clearing the air between them…so that they might part as friends, she thought with an empty numbness while, body and soul, what she ached for was his love.

'It's OK, I'll take it,' he insisted, when she made to lift the tray. But his smile was ruefully apologetic as he followed her back to the living-room. 'I'm not too good at this business of making amends—I just manage to sound nauseatingly—'

'Sandro, you don't have to make amends,' she blurted out, unnerved by the ferocity of the emotions churning within her. 'There's so much I have to explain, and which you probably won't believe…but in time, when you realise that article will never appear in print, you'll know I've told you the truth and—'

'If you're referring to your non-existent career as a journalist,' he said, placing the tray on the coffee-table, 'Babs has already taken care of that.'

'Taken care of it?' croaked Tessa.

He gave a diffident shrug, then sat down and looked up at her from coolly non-committal eyes. 'Yes. Yesterday I heard from Babs what I'd kept hoping to hear from you—and, God knows, I gave you enough opportunities!'

Feeling as if her mind was caught in an obstacle

course of contentious issues, Tessa reacted to the only point making a modicum of sense. 'You know!' she gasped. 'And that's why you decided to see me while you were in London.'

'I came to London solely to see you,' he stated expressionlessly, then glanced at the tray before him. 'I think you'd better pour—I'm feeling rather clumsy.'

With no single thought in her head now that was in any way coherent, Tessa sat down beside him on the sofa and, like one in a trance, began what proved to be a disastrous attempt to pour the coffee.

'Leave it,' he ordered brusquely, removing the pot from her dangerously trembling hand and returning it to the tray. 'The coffee can wait—but the talking can't.'

'Can't it? Is there really anything more to be said?' she asked bitterly, then shook her head, praying that she could last until he had left before going to pieces yet again. 'Of course there is!' she groaned in distraught reply to her own question. 'I went to Ireland for…for sneaky, underhand reasons! Sandro, I can't express how sorry I am for all the trouble that caused. I'll never understand why you couldn't just have come out with the fact that you knew, and given me the chance to explain… But I want you to know I'll always be grateful to you for coming here now and making it possible for us to part feeling perhaps a little less badly than we once did about one another.'

'A couple of weeks ago I contacted Babs and she refused to give me your address,' he said out of the blue, leaning back against the sofa as he spoke. 'She didn't openly refuse—but that's what it amounted to.'

Disconcerted by the way he had yet again swung off at a verbal tangent, Tessa simply closed her eyes and let his words wash over her.

'Something obviously made her relent, because she told me everything when she tracked me down in Florence the day before yesterday…after which she gave me her keys and told me I'd find you here.'

Tessa frowned, trying to remember if it had been the day before yesterday that Babs had left…whichever day it had been, no mention had been made of her seeing Sandro.

'So, here I am,' he stated wryly.

'And, as I said, I'm grateful you came—'

'Because we can now part again, but this time as friends?' he exploded savagely.

'Yes!' exclaimed Tessa, his rage instantly putting her on the defensive. 'And even if that isn't possible, at least some of the unpleasant misunderstandings between us have been cleared up.'

'Some?' he demanded harshly. 'What about the rest?'

'Sandro, the last thing I want is for us to start arguing,' Tessa protested huskily, defeat filling her as she felt the flickers of bitterness rekindling in her. 'I know there's no excuse for what I intended when I first went to Ireland. But I soon realised there was no way I could do such a thing…in my heart of hearts I'd always known it was wrong…I hadn't even been able to bring myself to read all those clippings I'd got together on you.'

'I'm not interested in all that!' he exploded.

'No, I don't suppose you are,' she whispered, flinching. 'I think it's best if you go now, Sandro.'

'Why? What are you so afraid of, Tessa?' There was bitter accusation in his tone. 'I'm the only man who's ever made love to you and I can't get the idea out of my head that you're a woman for whom lovemaking goes hand in hand with love. It was that question churn-

ing in my mind that drove me to try to get your address
from Babs.'

Tessa slumped back against the cushions, shaking her
head in protest. It was the bittersweet memories of their
lovemaking, creeping into her mind when she was at her
lowest, that she felt would one day destroy her fragile
sanity...yet it was those same memories that filled him
with guilt!

'Sandro, what possible difference can it make?' she
choked. 'It's over—finished! I was just as much to blame
as you—so stop wallowing in misplaced guilt!'

'What the hell's that supposed to mean?'

'It means that any guilt you feel should be over the
way you took your revenge, because whether or not I
was in love with you at the time is irrelevant. But, if
knowing I wasn't makes you feel any better—OK, I
wasn't!'

'There's one flaw in that tortuous bit of reasoning of
yours,' he snapped, 'in that guilt had little to do with it.
When I tried to get your address a couple of weeks ago,
I was under the impression that it was your journalistic
ambition that had brought you to my bed.'

'You what?' shrieked Tessa, sitting bolt upright.

'What the hell was I supposed to think?' he demanded, leaping up and scowling down at her. 'How
was I to know you'd given up any thought of that
damned article? When Angelica first told me about it, I
knew she wasn't lying—'

'How?' demanded Tessa, shaking uncontrollably.
'You know she's unbalanced, yet you believed her lies
when she rang you—'

'Whatever Angelica is, she isn't stupid,' he snapped.
'Merely by handing your file over to the receptionist,
she had a witness to its existence. And, as for her call

to me on the island, she went out of her way not to accuse you. Damn it, I'm pretty certain she planted the story herself, relying on me to leap to the conclusion I did. But Angelica's immaterial! It was *you* I wanted to hear the truth from! I wanted it voluntarily—not because you were cornered by a direct question! God, I did everything *but* ask you directly—yet who do I get it from? Babs!'

'I wanted to tell you…then I was too frightened to… I was so confused that I—'

'*You* were confused?' he roared. 'What the hell do you think *I* was? I've scarcely had a coherent thought since you turned up! And, while I may have slight problems with the written word, I had none whatsoever with spoken ones until I fell in love with you. And as for—'

'Sandro, stop!' gasped Tessa, her hands reaching out blindly towards him as she tried to catch her breath and at the same time cope with the words he couldn't have said.

'Damn it, no!' he groaned, grasping her by the hands and hauling her up and into his arms. 'You *can* love me!' he protested hoarsely, burying his face against her hair and threatening to squeeze the life from her with the frantic pressure of his hold. 'I know I was confused, but for a while I was certain you did love me…before I destroyed everything. Tessa, tell me you did—that you can again!'

The urgency with which his mouth found hers made answering impossible, but by then she was lost in the mind-numbing sweetness of being where she most belonged.

'The thought of never holding you like this again was driving me out of my mind,' he groaned in the instant before his lips again took hungry possession of hers.

As his kisses and the hoarse protestations interspersing them grew more frantic, Tessa clung to him, crying and laughing through the sweet fierceness of their bombardment. He couldn't have uttered those words—but he had! For so long he had confused and confounded her, yet all it had taken was one unguarded outburst of love to relegate all the pains and hurts to little more than a bad memory.

'I wanted to punish you so badly,' he muttered distractedly against her mouth, lifting her and sliding their bodies as one down on to the sofa. 'And it wasn't even decency that made me hesitate,' he confessed with husky breathlessness; 'it was the premonition that I'd end up hurting myself far more than I ever could you.'

'Sandro, please,' she choked, only the need to calm the terrible desperation in him holding her back from drowning completely in the magic of this miraculous moment. 'Stop!'

'I'll stop.' He gave a shuddering sigh as his arms slackened their suffocating hold, then drew back to gaze down at her from brooding, wary eyes. 'I understand… You can forgive me, but I treated you too badly for you ever to consider giving me a second chance.'

'Sandro, you understand nothing!' she protested. 'You were right! I could never make love to a man I didn't love. I've only ever made love with one man—the man I loved then, love now and will always love!'

There was a look of startled confusion on his face in the instant before his head dropped heavily against her shoulder.

'I… Oh, Tessa,' he muttered indistinctly, his arms readjusting themselves possessively around her. 'My mind's just seized up!' He suddenly lifted his head, a look of alarm on his face. 'Darling, you're shaking!'

'I…think it must be delayed reaction,' Tessa quavered. 'I can't believe any of this is really happening.'

'And you think I can?' he demanded in husky indignation, his hands not in the least steady as they cupped her face before he kissed her with breathtaking tenderness. 'Can you believe us?' he murmured dazedly. 'You name it, my darling, and we've managed to get it wrong…completely and earth-shatteringly wrong.'

'Do you really love me?' she whispered, her head spinning and her heart pounding as though it would burst.

'Love you?' he groaned shakily. 'I had to fight back the words every time we made love…I think I must have been fighting loving you almost from the moment I walked into that hotel lounge in Ireland and found myself being ogled by a child-woman, with a mouth like an angelic siren and eyes that were the most indiscreetly dirty and innocently beautiful I've ever seen…it was then that the instincts I'm always boasting about went into overdrive and I hadn't the faintest idea what they were telling me.'

'But you were hateful to me,' accused Tessa contentedly, no longer feeling tempted to pinch herself to make sure she wasn't dreaming as she snuggled closer to him. 'You told me I wasn't your type, despite your insatiable appetites!'

'I treated you in a manner I found appalling,' he admitted with a shudder, his arms tightening compulsively around her. 'I'd no idea I had it in me to behave like that…making all those crazy statements…threatening you! And that was before I'd even heard of that wretched file you'd started on me. When you told me what terrible taste you had in men, I could only agree wholeheartedly!'

'Except that when it comes to falling in love my taste is faultless,' she informed him dreamily.

'As is your taste in nightwear,' he chuckled teasingly, his fingers tracing the outline of the bear on her night-shirt, then deviating to devastating effect while he murmured huskily to her in Italian.

With a shivered gasp, she lifted her face to his, her arms winding invitingly round his neck. 'I suppose I'll have to start learning Italian as you have such problems with English,' she teased softly.

His shoulders tensed as he resisted the pull of her arms, but there was a sultry longing in his eyes that belied his action. 'I'll teach you,' he offered huskily, 'but only if you'll marry me.'

For a moment everything seemed to grind to a halt within her, and then even breathing became a struggle.

'Tessa, that's what love entails with me,' he pleaded passionately. 'A lifetime commitment...marriage... Tessa, can't you understand that with our record I'm almost afraid of blinking in case something else goes wrong? I—'

'Yes!'

'Yes, you can understand my fears that—?'

'Yes, I'll marry you!' she got out, then collapsed against him, ragdoll-limp with happiness.

His arms tightened suffocatingly around her. 'I think I suffered a minor heart attack while you were making up your mind,' he complained, his words whispering against her ear.

'I didn't need any time at all to make up my mind,' protested Tessa, laughter dancing through her happiness. 'It's just that you wouldn't let me get a word in...but I love you anyway.'

'I suppose that's a start,' he chuckled as he drew back

from her, his eyes twinkling as he attempted a menacing scowl. 'You do realise, don't you, that I've probably alienated your entire family—apart from Babs, that is?'

'Babs! If it hadn't been for her...' Her words choked to a halt.

'If it hadn't been for the magnificent Babs it would have taken us that much longer before we stopped behaving like a pair of idiots,' he whispered. 'But we'd have made it in the end, because I was finding life impossible without you.'

'It was unbearable...these past few weeks have been the most horrible of my life!' protested Tessa, clinging to him in panic as the ghost of those past agonies snaked through her. 'I didn't know myself any more. I kept bursting into tears without warning and having to avoid my poor mother because I knew it would break her heart to know how unhappy I was. And you needn't worry about her, or Charles—they'll both love you...so will Rupert, my half-brother.'

'And my parents will adore you,' he promised her huskily, while his hands embarked on a deliciously wicked bout of exploration in the vicinity of the teddy-bear.

'Are you sure?' she choked, grossly distracted by the electrifying effect of those purposefully roving hands.

'Positive. In fact, my mamma's likely to welcome you with open arms and tell you I'm not good enough for you,' he reassured her in a voice that was growing increasingly unsteady. 'Surely in those harrowing tales of my past I mentioned her having once confessed that, had she known she'd have only one child, she'd have passed me over for a precious baby girl?' With a soft growl of impatience he manoeuvred their frantically clinging bodies till they lay facing one another on the sofa. 'That's why I have this massive inferiority complex,' he ended with a breathlessly distorted chuckle.

'How am I ever going to believe a word you say?' she groaned through her own breathless laughter.

'You believe that I love you, don't you?' he demanded with husky indignation.

She nodded, incapable of words.

'And that it's forever?'

She nodded again, her lips nuzzling invitingly on his.

'So what's your problem?' he growled, but by then they had moved on to the next scene…the first in the rest of their life together.

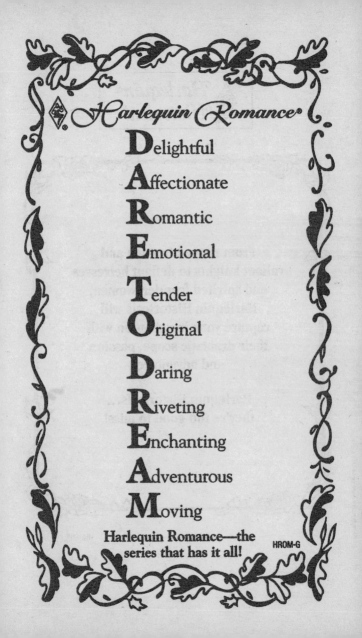

Harlequin Romance®

Delightful

Affectionate

Romantic

Emotional

Tender

Original

Daring

Riveting

Enchanting

Adventurous

Moving

Harlequin Romance—the
series that has it all!

HROM-G

Harlequin® Historical

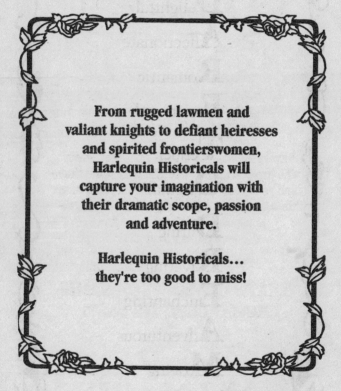

From rugged lawmen and
valiant knights to defiant heiresses
and spirited frontierswomen,
Harlequin Historicals will
capture your imagination with
their dramatic scope, passion
and adventure.

Harlequin Historicals...
they're too good to miss!

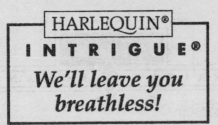

HARLEQUIN®

AMERICAN ◆ ROMANCE®

LOOK FOR OUR FOUR FABULOUS MEN!

Each month some of today's bestselling authors bring
four new fabulous men to Harlequin American Romance.
Whether they're rebel ranchers, millionaire power brokers
or sexy single dads, they're all gallant princes—and
they're all ready to sweep you into lighthearted fantasies
and contemporary fairy tales where anything is possible
and where all your dreams come true!

You don't even have to make a wish...
Harlequin American Romance will grant your every desire!

Look for Harlequin American Romance
wherever Harlequin books are sold!

HARLEQUIN SUPERROMANCE®

...there's more to the story!

Superromance. A *big* satisfying read about unforgettable characters. Each month we offer *four* very different stories that range from family drama to adventure and mystery, from highly emotional stories to romantic comedies—and much more! Stories about people you'll believe in and care about. Stories too compelling to put down....

Our authors are among today's *best* romance writers. You'll find familiar names and talented newcomers. Many of them are award winners—and you'll see why!

If you want the biggest and best in romance fiction, you'll get it from Superromance!

Available wherever Harlequin books are sold.

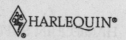

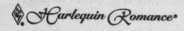

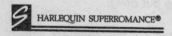